WAY OUT WEST

Way Out West

ISBN 978-0-9896812-3-0

Visit us online:
www.bigpulp.com
Facebook (Facebook.com/bigpulp)
Twitter (twitter.com/BigPulp)

Distributed by Ingram Periodicals

Ebook versions available from Amazon
and other online venues

Big Pulp Publications
BILL OLVER Editor/Publisher

Also by Bill Olver
Black Chaos II: More Tales of the Zombie (Editor, 2015)
Black Chaos: Tales of the Zombie (Editor, 2014)
The Kennedy Curse (Editor, 2013)
APESHIT (Editor, 2013)
Clones, Fairies & Monsters in the Closet (Editor, 2013)

WAY OUT WEST

Edited by
BILL OLVER

Big Pulp Publications

CREDITS

Diablo Seven © 2015 Terry Alexander
The Conservator © 2015 Cecelia Chapman
Have Time Machine, Will Travel © 2015 Harri B. Cradoc
The Showgirl and the Wendigo © 2015 Milo James Fowler
Junction, Texas © 2015 Joshua Gage
Boomer Boy, Now You're A Man © 2015 Walter Giersbach
Flesh, Soul, Money © 2015 DeAnna Knippling
Panning in Thin Air © 2015 Gerri Leen
Siege © 2015 Mike Loniewski
Chikcheeree © 2015 Paul Lorello
Above Snakes © 2015 John Medaille
The Two of Guns © 2015 John F.D. Taff
The Blood of Family © 2015 Joriah Wood

Cover illustration © 2015 **Luke Spooner**

Interior illustrations © 2015 **Ken Knudtsen**

TABLE OF CONTENTS

FLESH, SOUL, MONEY

by DeAnna Knippling

The wind blows across the prairie like a saw, cutting away the dead wood and turning everything into a sculpture. Nobody's there to see it but the rats and the snakes and the grasshoppers. Two men lie next to each other, both dead, both wearing identical outfits—cheap suits, bowler hats. The wind hasn't had time to work on them yet so it's up to the flies crawling over their coats and hats and leather boots. And flesh, of course.

The flies don't seem to be having much luck.

They were train robbers, Poindexter and Guillaume. The world was a richer place then: easier to steal. The treasure wasn't gold or silver but banknotes, but they still made a pretty good penny off robbing trains. They had got to the point where they hoarded the money like dragons hoarded gold anyhow, kept most of it in a series of underground caves.

To see them together you would have thought Poindexter was a businessman. Suit, bowler hat, tidy mustache. He had a kind of northeast feel to him but it was hard to say where from. Not New York, not Boston. Somewhere north of the Virginias. He was thick. So broad through the torso you would have been justified in calling him fat but that wasn't the important part. The important part was that he was strong as an ox and contained within himself reserves of both cleverness and cruelty. If you saw him apart from Guillaume, you'd think he looked like a thug. He wasn't from New England but from Manchester. He carried with him at all times a butterknife that had been carved into a very small saw. It was rusty and dull, couldn't hold an edge, and was stained with old blood in the crack between the handle and the blade. Other knives came and went but this one was with him always. Sometimes he whispered to it in his sleep.

Guillaume was—had been—one of the last of the old kind of fur trappers in Canada. Lived in the north wilds of Quebec. Fished through holes in the ice covered with skin tents. Eyes red from living with so much smoke. Smoked meat, cleaned furs, avoided his fellow man. Even now he wore a yellow leather jacket with a fringe of leather along the sleeves, kept his gray-and-white hair long and straggly, wore an eye patch. Stank of grease and smoke. Wore tied leather boots lined with rabbit fur. Had mice skulls in his pockets, which he would give to small children when bothered. He was enormous. Had been mistaken for a bear when he was younger and his hair was black.

The story was, he'd killed a whore who'd looked under the patch while he was passed out drunk. Somehow he'd known.

From our point of view, they were two men living in rougher, wilder times. From their point of view, they were watching the old ways die out and didn't much care for it. The trains came and went, carrying their burdens of men, men, always more men. Their women and children, too, respectable ladies who wanted social halls and churches and schools. The prairie echoed with the sound of hammers driving nails into pine boards. The wild men were dying out, and Poindexter and Guillaume didn't like the notion of it. So stealing from the trains wasn't just a pastime or a means of making a living. Neither one of them had need of money, as such. They hadn't been the kind of men who'd made money an equivalent to worth. No, the reason they stole money from trains was to announce to the world: *put your trust in this stuff and see what it gets you. It goes up in smoke.*

The problem was that the money had started getting hold of them. They had started out destroying the stuff, blowing up the trains, killing every man, woman, and child among them, driving off the cattle, prying open crates, hacking open flour sacks, pissing on clothes, and burning the money in a great whooping bonfire that drove the natives away for fear it would take the prairie and spread, which sometimes it did. But time had worn on, and the fires had grown smaller, then disappeared, and now they were at the point of carting the money away with them to their cave in Kansas.

But recently it had got even worse.

Here's what it had come to: Guillaume, being perhaps the more human of the pair, had taken a woman captive and had her on the saddle in front of him. Her hands were tied in front of her with rawhide. He'd soaked it and now it was drying out, getting tighter. The woman's hands were swollen and red but turning purple. Soon they'd be blue. She'd thrown herself off the horse a couple of times. Her face was beaten and bloody, just the way he liked it. She had a rag stuffed in her mouth.

Poindexter didn't like it. Oh, he liked hurting women as much as anybody, and he understood the need for a snack. It was the rag he didn't like. It wasn't torn off something. It wasn't robbed from one of the corpses, not even the woman's husband or little girl, lying dead on the scrub grass with the grasshoppers zinging through the air around them. It was a rag that Guillaume had brought with him, took out of his fringed leather coat, close to his chest. It spoke of a premeditated act. Of a plan.

"We'll kill her at the top of that ridge."

"We'll kill her when I say so." Guillaume stroked the woman's hair. It was matted with blood and dirt. Gold underneath, but there was no getting around that. "I took her, I kill her. You want a pussy puss of your own, you take one yourself."

"We'll kill her at the top of that ridge, I say. I don't want her polluting the place with her filth."

"I'm going to lay her down on top of the money when I do it.

Nice and slow. I like to listen to them singing."

The woman had had the horror beaten out of her, including most of her sense. And if she understood a word of what they were saying she couldn't say so, what with the rag stuffed in her mouth. At the moment, she was trying to swallow without getting the tail end of the rag, which tasted like rotten cheese, drawn down into her stomach.

They were monsters, Poindexter and Guillaume, no doubt about it. Let's not mince words here. They were murderers and monsters and train robbers. Let's not heroize them. I can understand the temptation to do so. We call some men heroes that aren't. Dig deep enough through the skin of anybody, you'll find something that's better left unseen, we know that. That's why we like our villains so much. They're closer to the truth. They show us what we already know: that, given the opportunity, we'll take every virtue and piss it away for gain. Sure, sure, the hero kills the villain but that's in stories, right? We know who the real hero is. It's all there to see.

But Poindexter and Guillaume are not those kinds of villains. They resist the snuffing out of humanity but that doesn't make them any better than monsters. It doesn't make them saints. It makes them monsters who like a particular spice of individualism to their meat.

Keep that in mind.

The train. It was stiflingly hot in the summer and rattletrap-cold in winter. The beds swayed at night and every creak, rattle, and snore could be heard through the curtains, and she didn't dare move lest she fall out of bed. She never slept, just laid awake and stared until she couldn't tell what was a dream and what was real. She dreamed of the dead, come back to haunt her. The only time they could find her was when she rode the rails, the unending thrum of the iron under them, the vibrations of the carriage, the smells of too many people shut up together for too long.

Karen was traveling with her family, that was, her husband and surviving child, back to Kansas. She'd lost a pair of twin boys born too small about six months ago. Since then she hadn't caught and was glad of it. Even though she wasn't popping them out the way "pioneer" women were expected to. The attitude in Kansas seemed to be that there was a continent to fill, and if she didn't help fill it, then that would mean there was more room for men from back East, the constantly flowing river of bodies that spread out from civilization like a plague. But after she'd lost the boys George hadn't touched her. It wasn't his way to weep but she felt the weight of the boys' loss in him, too.

She'd gone back to Massachusetts to stay with her mother while she recovered. Mattie played with Grandma while Karen wept, and huddled inside a wrapper of blankets, and drank cold tea and broth from trays, discreetly appearing and disappearing while life went on outside the narrow door to her childhood room. She wrote letters to George and prayed he hadn't done himself a mischief while she was gone. Now he'd come back East on business and it was time for her and Mattie to come home. His face was long and turned down at the mouth. It was a relief not to have to pretend to happiness with him.

Her stomach churned with every bump and lurch of the train. If she'd had to have ridden out here on a wagon train she would have killed herself after a week. As it was she clutched her hands together in her pearl-gray gloves, which seemed to show up dirt and stains even more than whites ones did. She hated trains. She hated *this* train. She hated the springs under the cotton batting, which was never thick enough. She hated the smell of ground-in dirt and rust underneath the powders and perfumes the women drenched themselves in. She hated the way she'd given Mattie opium to make her sleep, and she hated the way her child was so full of livelihood when she was awake. She hated the other passengers. They felt like fleas crawling through her clothes. Their eyes were on her always. If one person wasn't staring than another one was. She hated the sky, its unwearied blue that turned to contemplative black at night, so wide and yet so filled with stars. She wished for life in the city, with its heavy smells and gray skies and hopelessness. On the prairie one was constantly surrounded by people who told one to keep one's chin up, to always look on the bright side, etc., etc. She stared out the window and hoped that no-one would speak to her.

She didn't want to move forward. She didn't want to move on with her life. She didn't want to get back into the old routines. She didn't want to keep the books at the store. She didn't want to sweep out the dust or rub dishes dry.

She didn't want to deal with the business of living anymore. If only it hadn't been for Mattie she would have found release.

She was sure George felt the same.

The train rumbled. It was that time after sunset in which the world became haunted. The barren landscape flickered by. Stunted trees shadowed the course of a stream. They appeared in clumps, like the dots and dashes of a telegraph message. The grass turned gray, the sky leaden.

Her eyelids sank. She would sleep. She would sleep in the seat next to Mattie, and not in the bed. She would never sleep in the upper berth again. Her daughter was a warm presence beside her, curled up like a cat with her feet tucked under her blue wool coat. George sat opposite to her, studying her face. His mustache had grown longer, covering both lips and part of his chin. He looked as though he wanted to ask impossible questions. She closed her eyes.

The train jerked, and then she was flying.

The horses had been damaged. If they hadn't been damaged, they would have gone mad. But Guillaume knew the trick of it; he had a drill-tipped metal rod that he kept in his pack for just such an event. He was very matter-of-fact about it, not horrified in the least. He thought no more of a horse than you might think of a machine.

The three of them, the two monsters and their passenger, rocked along with the horses. The tack jingled dully, more like a pocketful of pennies than like bells. Your mind could only stay alert for so long in those conditions: the heat of the day, building after the dry, dewless chill of the night. The sweat on your skin evaporating before it had a chance to crawl, spiderlike, down your skin. Your identity fades, slips, transforms. Who are you, you wonder, as the heat ripples off the dirt road ahead.

Poindexter was aswim with souls, thousands and thousands of them. Human souls, bison souls, souls of small mice and large, ragged-furred rats. Horses, now. The souls of horses usually escaped him. Too restless. He shifted in his saddle; the smoothed, heavy cotton of his trousers squeaked against the leather. He wasn't *uncomfortable* with the woman, as such. Just Guillaume's interest in her.

Was it some perversion to do with the money? *Had* it been Guillaume who had made the decision—who had pushed, encouraged, manipulated—to save it, instead of destroying it? He, Poindexter, was the manipulator. He, Poindexter, knew that his function in their duo was to manipulate. He was the talker that contained the hidden threat. Guillaume was brute force that contained a direct cunning: and yet this plan, this plot of his seemed to contain manipulations. Hidden threats. *Had* Guillaume become Poindexter, and Poindexter, Guillaume?

When you get off a horse this kind of thinking fades; you know who you are. Guillaume knew that this mindlessness came from the properties of the body he currently inhabited, that this strange wandering of thought was not madness as much as some kind of surreality constructed over the gaps in his idle thoughts. It was like dreaming, a torturous dream inflicted by one's own flesh. He had inflicted such dreams on others. He had used the properties of the flesh to drive men mad, and take their souls. That it was happening to him seemed an indication that he was, himself, being infiltrated. Manipulated.

Violated.

Had *he,* Poindexter, been damaged? Had Guillaume taken the rod, pushed his eye gently to the side, and drilled into his skull? It was not beyond the realm of possibility.

"Guillaume," he said.

Guillaume grunted.

"Kill her or I will. Now. Before we get to the caves. This is wrong and you know it."

Guillaume spat on the ground, turning his head so he wouldn't foul the woman's dress. Poindexter felt the hairs on his arms raise, even in this heat. The grass around them sniggered in long ripples across the prairie. The wind gusted over his skin and brought up gooseflesh.

"Won't," Guillaume said. "You had better leave it alone, my friend."

"Tell me what you're doing."

"Saving for later."

"You've never done that before."

"That's true, I haven't. Now shut it before I knock you off that horse."

Before, he had always been able to read Guillaume's mind, as it were. They had been of one mind, one purpose. And now they were not. *Who* had decided to keep all the money? Had it been him? He couldn't remember. There was a stone in the caves of his mind. The intricate caves. And in order to remember he would have to roll back the stone.

And then no amount of damage would stop the horses from bolting.

The train screamed. It was a nightmare of sound, pain, and disorientation. Karen flew through the air like a doll, bouncing off the seat backs, the roof, other passengers. Her world mercifully turned to blackness. Her daughter died, shall we say, instantly. At any rate she never woke from her opium-induced slumber. Karen's husband, George, had the grief of remaining conscious, pinned to his seat with a wooden pole from the underside of a folded-up upper berth, meant to help the passengers steady themselves as they walked. His guts had been punctured, a nice slow death as far as Poindexter was concerned. George tried to pull the pole out of his flesh but he lacked the moral strength to do so. He tried not to despair; every quiver in his guts was like a knife. He wished for one last sight of his daughter or wife, although such a thing would have hurt him worse than he could have imagined. He was a good man.

The night flowed in around the train car. When the train finally fell silent but for the sobbing and fear, the only sounds were of Guillaume and Poindexter, having tied their horses at a nearby farmhouse in preparation for their adventures. They passed from car to car, feeding.

They supped on the rich; they feasted on the poor.

There was no money on this train, not as such—only what the individual passengers carried, which was hardly worth the time it took to paw through their pockets. They bypassed pocket watches, jewelry, false teeth, ivory canes, etc. In times of scarcity they would have considered taking a silver-framed locket containing the very picture of love lost, or a child's toy *sans* child, or any other object infused with the essence of a poignant memory. They would have hoarded.

They would have *taken some for later.*

But this was not a time of scarcity—was it? They were fully fleshed; they ate well; the world was what it was; the men from the East flowed, they oozed, they squelched. There was plenty, even if there were others of their kind mucking about, to go around.

Poindexter sipped Mattie's last heartbeats, then pressed his lips to Karen's. She was lovely, as bruised as an apple, and mercifully unaware of him. One brush against her lips—one taste of the pain awaiting her—and he laid her carefully outside the train car, to await her wakening.

Perhaps she would be well enough to walk. Or to run. They could afford to take the chance of losing her. *They could even let her go.* To spread the horror. To make it ripe.

Guillaume saw it, of course. He saw the tender way Poindexter, having overrun his human form, lifted her gently out of the train car and laid her on the ground. Meanwhile Guillaume chewed the twisted wreck of the engine, sucking out its soul from the metal marrows, licking its blood and steam. Poindexter had been acting oddly lately. He'd been taking all that money. Hiding it in the cave as though it were somehow useful or precious to them.

Would it lure prey to them? The humans pursued money. He hadn't protested, because Poindexter had it in him to be clever, to see things that could and ought not be seen. He could see surprises. Guillaume took a solid pleasure out of Poindexter's plans, because Poindexter revealed all the surprises ahead of time. To know the future made Guillaume feel godlike. Not for very long at a time. But it was nevertheless a pleasure he could not obtain on his own, not from the destruction of any number of humans, or any number of betrayals, or any number of the uses of machinery.

In his way, Guillaume was worried about Poindexter, who seemed to have split in two: the Poindexter who knew about the money, and the Poindexter who didn't. Madness was a human occupation. He ought to kill Poindexter and free him from the flesh but who knew when he'd find his way back to Guillaume again? Or how angry he would be when he did.

No. He would have to find another way.

He looked at Poindexter, picking through the train car. When Poindexter was done Guillaume planned to pull apart the sleeping berths. Their smooth, varnished wood was sensuous on his tongue, full of hushed sex, illness, crazed nightmares, guilt.

If only he had been happier in his life, he would have avoided all this. He was not like Poindexter, he'd been born human. But he had despaired, and in his despair, opened himself to influences out in that long, lonely wilderness. He had longed to surround himself with men, with the signs and creations of men. And the hungry ones had found him there. He had opened himself further and further…now he was the kind of thing that machines despaired of, the ender of their lush mechanical essences, their nightmare.

Poindexter did not truly understand what possessed Guillaume. A predator evolves with its prey; this Guillaume had always been aware of, even in Quebec. Poindexter hunted for a different kind of prey than did Guillaume, and found him foreign. Poindexter had come from the Old World, and had Old World ways and knowledge and cleverness, for hunting men.

Guillaume had evolved with the New World, had been possessed by it. Under his coat he was metal, a man being remade as metal. Soon it would begin to cover his face, to invade even the semblance of humanity that remained to him.

And then Poindexter would go, and he would be alone.

If Poindexter wished to savor the woman, Guillaume reasoned, then she must be good prey. She contained some essence, some perfume. Within his coat he had a rag that he had carried with him for years, not out of any meaning, but because he needed a rag. When he had started becoming metal he carried it with him, he sniffed at the stink of it in order to remind himself what humanity smelled like. At first it had stunk…then it had smelled of meat…now it was cloth, nothing more. At first he had been able to resist the horror of the loss—the loss of his stink, which he would have been glad of, when he hunted beaver and elk and rabbit!—but of late it made him gnash his teeth at night, with the groan of strained metal.

He pulled out the rag, shoved it in the woman's mouth, and threw her over his shoulder. She weighed nothing. His belly grumbled. He had held himself back, had not eaten his fill.

He would eat this woman, and take on her essence. He would take on the essence of her that was full of fear of *his* old, human essence. Her fear would teach him how to be human again.

He would eat her; they would burn the money; all would be right again.

Reaching the limestone cavern, a couple of hundred miles to the southeast, meant they had to keep the woman alive for days on end, a tiresome business that Guillaume had had more experience with than Poindexter. Guillaume knew how to hunt things that weren't human, and insisted they do so: both to prevent their being followed as well as to spare the woman the distress of cannibalism. He had tried to explain this to Poindexter, whose instincts pointed toward causing distress rather than sparing it, but Poindexter only turned his head away. "You're the one who wants to keep her alive. What does it matter what I think?" Bitter, resentful. Soon, Guillaume promised himself. Soon it would be over. But the anxiety within his increasingly metal mind sounded like a spring, twisted, its metal shrieking its deformity as it was forced into actions it had never been created for.

He could hear small pings, the ticking of a clock in his head, which was really the movement of gears and springs and ratchets. The horror was that he found the ticking soothing. In dreams he found himself contemplating entering the guts of a city, lurking below it, preying on the machines that lay below the surface, helpless, unguarded. That which possessed him was not only rebuilding his body, but his soul.

He roasted a brace of rabbits over a small fire—waste not, want not—and lurched with a residual, mad nausea every time he rose to turn the green-wood spit. Poindexter stared at the women, smacking his lips, as she watched the skinned animals over the haze of coals. Earlier, when the flames had been high, she had hummed to herself, rocking back and forth with her arms around her knees. A lullaby.

She watched the rabbits roasting because she was hungry, although their glistening bodies looked suspiciously like cats, their ears having been removed by Guillaume when he skinned them, apparently using the back edge of his right pinkie, as though it were a knife.

She'd watched the flames because something had whispered to her, out of the flames. Not *to* her, as such. But whispering. A cacophony of whispers, as though she were at a theater where the curtain had been down too long. She could not understand the words, but she felt the emotions of the whisperers. The emotion was longing—dissatisfaction. A sense of restlessness. A sense that if only one tried a little harder, worked a little more loyally, one would find *it*. Whatever *it* was. Not family, not friends. *It* could not be found in drink, although drink could suppress the need to find *it* for a while, as could—she noted curiously, for she had never really enjoyed it—sex. Food could comfort those without *it*, and…

…Karen stared into the flames and tried to remember when she had first heard the whispering. Before the train wreck, or after? She could not sort it out, but she suspected, by the time the flames had died down, that she had *been* one of the whisperers, back East.

At the time her despair and longing for death had felt to be much more than dissatisfaction. Her *sons* had died, and there was nothing to be done for it. The other lives around her had had no meaning. A well of resilience within her had been drained, profoundly and permanently drained—or so she'd thought.

But, looking into the fire, and sensing the wash of dissatisfaction coming through the fire, she felt as though a small trickle of hope were coming back into her: a small spring in the pit of her despair.

It hurt.

Which was, after months of numb, deadening despair, an unfamiliar sensation.

The landscape changed around them, from the open, gray-dry prairie, to the rising crests of the Ozarks. The world was greener, a little less abandoned, although not exactly populated. Through the heavy trees they could glimpse a disarrangement of the natural order: farms cut out of woodlands, thin trails of smoke, a dog barking, a double-line of dirt through a meadow. Nothing like Kansas City or the thick polluting scabs of civilization out East. Still, these small things reminded both Poindexter and Guillaume that a world was coming to an end. Wilderness was dying. The *idea* of wilderness was dying, here, as they watched.

Nevertheless the things they carried inside themselves were able to warp the world a little in their favor. They remained unseen.

To Karen, the whispering was becoming louder, almost deafening. She shivered constantly.

"Is it sick?" Poindexter asked. "Dying? We could kill her—it—now, you know."

Guillaume urged his horse a little faster. At the end they were galloping up the trail to the cave, with its low, gaping, sloppy kind of mouth. Their control over the horses was starting to slip; the horses foamed at the mouth and trembled with exhaustion. Even in their mentally deadened state they seemed to feel fear.

Inside Guillaume's head was a kind of tearing sound. He would start to think a thought, and be unable to finish it:

You are losing your—
After the woman—
Too late, it's—
The machine is—

The horse ran blindly up the crushed-rock slope and nearly brained him on the mouth of the cave. It refused to stop when he leaned back and jerked on the reins but turned sharply, throwing the two of them off. Guillaume's horsemanship seemed to have left him. The woman skidded across the fallen rock. He had stopped tying her hands together; she had become catatonic, unable to eat or speak, or do little more than breathe. In the end he had removed the rag and stuffed it down the fetid front of her dress, in case she choked on it. Now she lay stunned, perhaps dying.

He got his boots under him. His spurs jingled, or else it

was his soul. Poindexter rode up behind him, looking down on him with the sun at his back. Guillaume could feel the sneer on Poindexter's lips. Broken, everything was broken. He picked up the woman. On her lips was a smile, a horrid, evil smile. But there was no time to consider it.

The woman suddenly gasped, stretching out full length with her hands over her head, arching her back. Cloth ripped. He should have left her bound. She was trying to get away.

"Help me," Guillaume said.

The woman thrashed and kicked in his arms, not frantically or consciously. Her eyes were still closed. She was a dreamer swimming to the surface. Suddenly she had flipped out of Guillaume's arms and was on her feet. She brushed her filthy dress down. Her blond hair lay lank on her shoulders in clumps. They should have raped her. They should have *killed* her.

She rippled with strength. Her dress was splitting down the seams, through her lower arms and across her torso, showing a rotten yellow slip underneath, stained a garish orange, the color of illness, not of wholesome blood. She opened her eyes and they glowed blue.

Poindexter was taken back to his younger days, in a place you might call Hell, if you were particularly unimaginative about other realms than these. He had once tried to torture something stronger and nastier than he was, and had run squeaking in terror when it had burst out of the human form it had been wearing. He wanted to bow. He wanted to beg for mercy. He wanted to run.

Poindexter's horse reared. It was a choice between trying to stay astride or rolling free. He shoved away from the horse, stumbled, then did something small, and brave, and nearly human as the woman turned toward his companion, his friend: he attacked her.

He threw himself on her back. With a flick of his wrist he had a razor out from his sleeve and open. He slashed it across the woman's throat. Then he flew through the air, rolling down the slope, keeping his head close. He lost the razor, whose specialty was cutting through hope. The world flashed: sky…rock…trees…

He hit a boulder and stopped, then woozily got to his feet. The woman staggered into the cave. If she was bleeding he couldn't see it. But he had distracted her from Guillaume, so it was enough.

The whispers pulled Karen forward, step by step. Although she still had no idea what was pulling her—what was happening to her—it was at the exact moment that she walked through the mouth of the cave that Guillaume calculated the truth.

He followed her, jingling and creaking. His limbs felt heavy, solid, unstoppable—but that was a lie, he knew. Rust seemed to creep through his limbs.

Guillaume entered the cave behind the woman as though hypnotized. His gait stiff and staggering, the fringe of his leather jacket swinging wildly. His friend had been captured, enslaved.

Poindexter ran up the hill and threw himself onto Guillaume's back, trying to knock him over. Guillaume rocked forward, but regained his balance. Poindexter slid off his back. The fringe of the leather jacket swayed.

"Guillaume," he said. "Stop."

But Guillaume had lost his thoughts entirely. His own transformation had overtaken him.

Poindexter jogged around his friend and struck him in the face. It was a powerful punch but did nothing. Guillaume came on like a juggernaut. Poindexter looked over his shoulder: the woman was heading directly toward the cache of money.

Then he knew, too, what was happening.

"My friend, my friend," he laughed. "You were right. I should have burnt the money. I should have burnt it. I should have made it into a holocaust."

Guillaume's eye patch had slipped. His eye was no longer

human, but shining copper. And the eyelid under it was drooping away, showing the shining brass underneath.

It was too late. For how long had it been too late, and he had not known?

Karen found the false wall along the side of the cave and stepped through it. It led down a crevice, a thing not made by human hands but marked by them. The walls narrowed. She turned sideways but it became apparent that she could not proceed further.

The whisperers needed her. She needed them. She scraped off the rags of her dress and shoved herself a little further forward.

A crack of light shone down on her from above: the last place, the last test, the last question.

Would she rise to Heaven? Or enter the depths of Hell?

Her flesh split and she shoved herself further into the crack, leaving her humanity behind.

She felt renewed.

Poindexter ate the dress. The flesh, too. He followed the woman deeper and deeper into the place where he had stashed the money. Banknotes...a dragon's hoard of banknotes.

The stone had been rolled away from his memory. *He* had stolen the money, not Guillaume. He hadn't known why he'd done it at the time, only that it was important that he do so. Now he knew. He knew that he'd been used. His sanity, his strength had been stripped away.

The razor was gone but he still had the butterknife, carved into the shape of a small saw.

Goodness would not triumph here. There would be no possibility of justice. Or hope. It was just a matter of what kind of despair would gain a foothold here. You know how this goes as well as I do—the outcome, if not the details. But Poindexter did not.

He thought the knife would answer the thing that possessed the woman, with the condensed horror of all his crimes against humanity. For there to be crimes against humanity, there must be humanity, after all. He would fight for monstrosity, for whispered stories in the dark. He would fight, not for justice, but for the bright spark of fear.

The slitlike cavern widened. He caught up to her as her flickering form reached the bags of money he'd madly insisted on bringing in. The canvas bags could have held grain, or potatoes but instead held…not souls, but something more primitive than that. Starved things, full of want. Mewling growth that, properly fed, could have become men, or monsters, but were instead a kind of blind force, without salvation, damnation, or choice.

He stabbed her with the knife. Shoved it into her midriff, and ground it in deep, twisting it, ripping the blade back, and shoving it in deeper. His hands knew what to do, even though his eyes tried to deceive him, and tell him that the woman was nothing but a ghost.

Blue fire burst out of her flesh and spilled over his hand and up his arm. He screamed in pain. Pain! He had not felt it for a long time, a very long time. But he kept sawing away at her innards.

She turned toward him. It was a motherly face. A loving one. She must have been a good mother, he thought, before the possession had taken her. Limned with blue fire, her face seemed filled with compassion, all-giving, all-providing. She took his wrist and he let go of the knife, his *first* knife, the one filled with the most savory souls he'd collected, the killers. Every true monster he'd taken was contained in that knife.

It burned with a puff, and she brightened for a moment— then was whole again.

Poindexter knew despair. His human form dissolved like piss running down his leg.

She walked into the first pile of bags, and a ghostly blue fire surrounded both her and the bags, like burning whiskey.

As the starved spirits were consumed, they grew, spreading from pile to pile until all their hoarded treasure was aflame.

Poindexter felt something pulling him from behind, and yielded to darkness.

Karen felt the well of her despair fill, overbrimming, with need. The more she consumed, the less she despaired…but the more she hungered. That's the way of money, though, isn't it? Mattie and George were dead, their souls consumed by a different type of monster. That pain remained. The despair—that she hadn't loved them, that she hadn't been good enough for them, that she had wanted to die—*that* was banked fire, however, and she would do anything to keep it from being stirred back to life.

But the money was consumed, all too quickly. She needed more.

Guillaume dragged Poindexter out of the caves by his tail. His clothes, his flesh had sloughed away. His mind had become clearer and more distant, less irrational.

And yet he dragged Poindexter free of the flames before he could be consumed. As the passage narrowed, he rebuilt himself to fit through the available space. It slowed him but not much, and of course Poindexter, with his sinuous, oozing body, could fit through the narrowest of gaps already.

"My souls," Poindexter moaned. "My knife. My souls."

They reached the larger cavern. Guillaume ducked as he exited the cave mouth. The horses were gone.

Guillaume rebuilt himself as an engine, like a train but with rolling treads. You wouldn't have recognized him, but he was a kind of tank, carrying what looked like a thick rope of London fog, only with claws and teeth—Poindexter's true form. They trundled off along the prairie.

It wasn't as though the two of them had *invented* money. Or that it had never before possessed a soul. But they *were* there, at the turning point.

At *a* turning point.

Guillaume stopped at a stream to drink, crossed it, and rolled away, puffing steam.

She catches them out on the gray prairie, in a place so remote that their bodies will not be found for generations, and will be mistaken for something other than corpses when they are.

She descends out of the air like glowing blue smoke. Guillaume rolls faster but becomes stuck in wire—barbed wire. No matter how he changes he cannot seem to get it off him. The wire is already one of *her* servants, and will not release him.

"Go!" he orders Poindexter, and turns to fight her to the last.

Poindexter, now rested, bursts into the air but makes the mistake of looking back. Guillaume is frozen, wrapped in wire but no longer struggling against it. His metallic body softens and changes, not to flesh but to a kind of waxy material, clothed in a cheap gray suit with a bowler hat, the kind of thing Poindexter wears but ineffably different.

Then the thing turns its attention to Poindexter, and he falls from the sky, stumbling on stiff shoes that are supposed to look like leather but aren't, and that already pinch his feet. The thing's gaze beats down on his back. He can barely crawl but drags himself toward Guillaume.

His flesh is hardening, stiffening. At first hot and flexible, now it's cooling into immobility. He collapses next to Guillaume. His bowler hat remains firmly affixed to his head.

The two men are indistinguishable now, but for Guillaume lying on his back, and Poindexter on his stomach.

The thing over them turns Poindexter over and straightens Guillaume's limbs. Now they *are* indistinguishable. Replaceable, interchangeable.

She sips their souls, absorbing their longing and changing it to the dull buzz of dissatisfaction. They are large souls, old and rich, but she's able to reduce them to simpler stuff, more easily digested.

Their faces melt a little in the sun, but that's all right. The flies buzz futilely around them. It would be up to the sun and the wind to erode them: but they would be safely buried in the soil before they had been worn away, and only exposed generations later, when a backhoe went to dig out part of a hillside for a landfill and discovered the plastic manikins already buried there.

Karen turns East.

DiABLO SEVEN

by Terry Alexander

Sullivan reined the gelding to a stop. He stared through the early evening twilight at the two men fussing around the cookfire.

"The boys will be here shortly. They'll want hot food and coffee." The older man with the battered hat and chin whiskers busied himself with a large stew pot.

"Yes, Sir." The younger man added sticks to the fire, under the oversized coffee pot. "We'll be ready."

"Hello the camp." Sullivan tugged the leather throng from the .45's hammer, and twisted the grip to one side. He didn't think the two men were troublemakers, but on the frontier it paid to be sure. "Coming in for a cup of joe."

The old timer pulled a rifle from the wagon and cocked the hammer. Sullivan grinned. He wasn't the only one who believed in being cautious.

"Come ahead, if you're friendly," the older man yelled.

Sullivan eased the gelding forward. "Saw your fire." He climbed from the saddle. "Don't see many wagons out in this country." Dry brittle grass crunched under his worn boots.

"Get the man some coffee." The older man moved to the far side of the fire. His finger curled over the trigger of the old single shot Hawken. "We're driving a herd of brush cattle up to Abilene. I'm G. W. Wishbo…call me Whiskers, that's Mushgrove, cook's louse."

"Mr. Wish…Oh," Mushgrove grunted as the old man kicked his leg.

"Get the man some coffee," Whiskers repeated.

Mushgrove passed him a bent tin cup filled to the brim. "Here you go. Hope it's to yore likin."

"Thanks, Mushgrove." Sullivan sipped the brew.

"I didn't catch yore name, Stranger." Whiskers held the rifle at Sullivan's middle.

"O. P. Sullivan." He squatted next to the fire and refilled the cup. "What's G. W. stand for?" Sitting the cup on the stones surrounding the fire, Sullivan slipped the leather strap over the hammer.

"George Washington, yours?" Whiskers eased the hammer down on the rifle, leaning it against the front wagon wheel.

Sullivan shrugged. "Orange Pekoe."

"Lord Almighty, what kind of a handle is that?" The old timer filled a tin plate with beans and passed it to Sullivan.

"Maw crossed the ocean, with her daddy, when she was a little tyke. Grandpa was always partial to tea, and that appreciation rubbed off on her." Steam rose from the plate. "I was the first born after her and Daddy married. Grandpa said she drank tea everyday when she was carrying me so Dad named me Orange Pekoe."

"That's a good yarn." Whiskers smiled. He filled a cup and sipped the strong brew. "My pappy named me after the first president."

"Stands to reason." Sullivan chewed a mouthful of beans. "Yore trailing brush cattle to Kansas. Bet it was rough going rounding them up."

Mushgrove nodded. "We spent six weeks gathering this bunch. They're not trail broke yet."

"See anything of the Seven bull the Mexicans talk about?"

"Diablo Seven." Whiskers refilled the empty cup. "Saw him one morning at daybreak. I was taking care of personal business before I started breakfast when he appeared at the edge of camp, had a woman with him. He just stared at me for a few seconds, then she crawled up on his back and he trotted off into the darkness."

"Heard he travels with a young handsome woman." Sullivan drained the cup and tossed it to Mushgrove. "Some of the local ranchers have put a two hundred dollar bounty on that animal."

"Couldn't tell her age. You take my advice and leave that one alone. Diablo Seven killed five men." Whiskers wagged his finger at Sullivan. "No need to make it six."

"Gosh, Mr. Wish—I mean Mr. Whiskers. Two hundred dollars is a lot of money." Mushgrove dropped the cup in the washtub.

A smile touched Sullivan's lips. "I've heard he's the biggest longhorn that ever walked the earth, thick at the shoulders and hips, wide black head with a speckled body, with a white seven in his forehead. The Mexicans say the earth trembles when he runs."

"Seems like you studied this varmint right smart." Whiskers shook his head. "Several good men have tried to lay that bull low. Some of our crew had a go at him and came up short. That devil's packing the skulls of the last two men he killed."

"How is that possible? A bull ain't got no hands." Mushgrove shook his head.

"He runs folks through with those long horns," Sullivan said. "He hooked a fella in the back of the head last year, right at the base of the skull. He whipped around and tore the head right off the feller's body. Don't know how he got the other."

"Well, he's got two skulls now, one on each horn. The left one's trailing about six inches of backbone," the old man interrupted. "Only a crazy man looks for that kind of trouble."

Mushgrove nodded. "I ain't ever seen two hundred dollars at one time."

"A man can die for a lot less." Whiskers frowned. "There ain't any such thing as easy riches."

Sullivan scratched his whiskered jaw. "That critter was born in a cemetery on Dia de los Muertos. Cow dropped her baby on a killer's grave. An evil spirit came through the earth and crawled into the calf through the nostrils."

"That's nothing but an old wives' tales folks tell their kids to keep them in line." Whiskers waved his hands in disgust.

"The Mexicans say the evil spirit makes the bull kill." Sullivan rose to his feet. "I see dust coming this way. Reckon it's your crew." He placed the plate on the tailgate. "Thanks for the grub. You ain't a bad cook."

"Wish you'd stick around and tell them others that," Whiskers snapped. "They're an ungrateful bunch, always complaining."

"I'd better get moving." Sullivan stretched his back, as he walked toward the gelding. "How long's it been since you've seen Seven?"

"A week, maybe ten days ago, fifty miles south of here." Whiskers yanked the hat from his head and scratched his bald dome. "How are you gonna nab that thing when so many others failed?"

Sullivan grabbed the saddle horn, he swung his leg over the saddle and settled into the worn leather. "Got a Sharpe's Carbine. Figure I'll take Seven at long range." His spurs touched the gelding's flanks. The animal moved forward slowly.

"You ain't gonna get any long distance shots in that brush," Whiskers shouted to the departing figure. "That bull will be on you before you know it."

"Bye, Mr. Orange. You be careful now," Mushgrove yelled through his cupped hands.

Sullivan huddled by a small campfire. He left the chuck wagon five days ago, and encountered an outrider from one of the ranches yesterday. He'd lucked on a clearing with a small stream and good grass. Although it was early afternoon, he decided to camp for the night. He and the gelding both needed the rest.

He gnawed a tough strip of beef jerky, washing it down with the last of his coffee. Sullivan leaned back on his saddle and gazed at the far horizon. He thought back to Ohio and the days before the war.

Jocelyn's face appeared in his memories. Sweet innocent Jocelyn with strawberry hair, her nose covered with freckles. The most beautiful girl he'd ever known. Her smile could set a strong man's heart to fluttering, her green eyes always held a mischievous sparkle. They planned to marry when he returned home.

During the early days, her letters arrived every week. He wrote back whenever he could. But then things got hard and the letters stopped. He sat up and gazed into the fire, hoping the dancing flames would chase the visions away. Her face wouldn't leave him.

When the war ended he returned to Ohio, hoping to rekindle their romance. He found her headstone in the local cemetery. Scarlet fever had swept through the county during his absence and claimed many of the inhabitants. Jocelyn never mentioned the sickness in her letters. She died less than a year after joined the Union army.

He shook his head, desperate to drive the memories away. The image of her face crystallized into greater detail. Jocelyn died alone and scared. The tombstone was for show, she didn't have a proper burial with sweet words spoke over her. She was thrown into a ditch and burned to ash, along with thirty other unfortunates.

The afternoon passed on to dusk. A movement along the western horizon caught his attention. Jocelyn's face vanished in an instant. He climbed to his feet, staring at a grove of stunted trees.

"What the hell?" he mumbled.

A huge shape moved into the dying light. Wide flaring horns glowed in the twilight, the twin skulls, at the base of each horn, slack jawed and laughing.

"Diablo Seven." Sullivan crept to his saddle, tugging the buffalo rifle from the worn leather scabbard. Nervous fingers groped in the saddle bag for shells. He worked the breech and shoved a bullet in the barrel. "Old Whiskers didn't think I'd get a shot at you, and there you are just as pretty as you please."

He flipped the sight up and squinted down the barrel. He saw the glow playing around the horns for an instant. A young woman stepped from the trees and stared in his direction. She jumped onto the brute's back, and the pair disappeared, swallowed by the gathering dusk.

"Where did you go, Seven?" he mumbled. "Where are you?"

The sharp snap of broken tree limbs echoed through the stillness. Sullivan tried to determine the direction of the creature's movements, the dense growth redirected the sounds back at him.

The Longhorn burst through the thick scrub growth. Its blood red eyes glowed in the weak light, thick mist billowed from its nostrils. The skulls jiggled with the monster's every step.

Sullivan froze, his feet rooted to the ground. He stared in dumb fascination as the creature raced toward him. At the last instant, the need for self-preservation made him leap for safety.

White hot agony blossomed in his side. He struck the brute with his fists, feeling thick corded muscles beneath the thick hide. It lifted him in the air and flung him away like a cat worrying a mouse. Sullivan landed in a thorn patch. His gelding's panicked whinny came to him before he passed out.

Sunlight streamed through the leafy growth, striking his eyes. A gentle breeze whistled through the spindly limbs. He moved a hand to shade his eyes. Pain lanced through his side and convinced him to lay still.

"See yore awake, young feller." An old woman wearing dirty, patched clothes leaned over the campfire. Thick grime covered her face, an old Confederate hat perched atop her drab gray hair. "You tangled with Seven last night. Damn wonder he didn't kill you."

"He tried awful hard." Sullivan struggled to sit up.

"Don't tear them bandages loose, you damned idjit. You lost a lot of blood. That wound gets to leaking again I might not be able to stop it. Can't have you dying right now, Millie's got plans for you." She poked a stick in the fire. "She's out scrounging up some medicine for you."

"Who's Millie?"

"My daughter." The gray head nodded. "Horn didn't penetrate your gut; think you could handle a little coffee?"

"Think so." Sullivan gritted his teeth, as pain radiated through his side. He braced his back against a small sapling. "Where's my horse and rifle?"

"Yore hoss is gone to parts unknown, broke away when the bull attacked. Yore rifle is over yonder, stock's busted." She filled a bent cup with hot liquid and passed it to Sullivan.

He blew the steam away. "Who are you?"

"Dora Plunkett. My husband Langdon served with the Georgia Seventh Infantry," she said, proudly. "We came here when things started going bad for the Confederacy. What's yore handle?"

"Sullivan." His face wrinkled in disgust, as he sipped the brew. "This stuff's awful."

"My own special mixture, ground up mesquite seeds mixed with the coffee, adds a little sweetness to it. One of the first lessons I learned when we got here." A gap toothed smile split Dora's face.

"Seven doesn't bother you?" Sullivan tilted the cup to his lips.

"No reason why he should, he's my husband. Didn't catch yore first name." Dora stuffed a pipe with rough cut tobacco. She pulled a small stick from the fire and puffed the smoke to life.

Sullivan licked his lips. "Orange Pekoe." He swallowed a hard lump in his throat. "What do you mean yore husband?"

"Lord Goodness, what kind of a name is that?"

A girl with raven black hair and dark eyes walked silently into the camp. Her cast-off clothing fit her like a glove. Dirt and grime covered her dusky skin.

"Millie, this is Orange, he's the one that been stumbling around here for the last couple days, hunting yore daddy."

"Me and daddy done the hunting." She tossed Dora a cloth bag. "Found some snake and mustard root. Boiled down they should make a good poultice." She turned to Sullivan. "Wish papa would have killed you." Her words dripped venom.

"Millicent, be nice. This fella is gonna be the daddy of yore child." Dora dumped the roots into a small pot. "Now you apologize to our guest."

"I didn't invite him here." She squatted on her haunches and filled a tin cup with coffee. "Seven's going to the water hole, figure he'll hit the sweet grass on the south meadow and circle back this way."

"What in the hell do you mean? I ain't any child's father." Sullivan's lips whitened as he tried to rise.

"Don't get that hole to bleeding again," Millie shouted.

Sullivan slowly lowered himself to the ground, his face white and pasty. "What's going on."

"My daddy was George Plunkett. Mesicans killed him down below the border some years back. Little over five years ago me, Mama and Briscoe found an old longhorn ready to drop. We tied the cow over daddy's grave. Mama said some big words while she was straining to squirt the little one out. When she birthed the calf, daddy's spirit crawled out of the grave and down its throat." She drained the foul brew. "Maw, where's Briscoe?"

"He's out looking for this jasper's horse."

"Keep enough water on them roots so they boil to a thick ointment." Her dark eyes settled on Sullivan. "If he don't find your horse, Orange, we'll have to carry you out of here. Sure hope you're worth all this trouble."

"You folks are plum loco." Sullivan stared at the young woman. "You honestly believe that Seven is yore daddy?"

"Yore kinda slow, ain't you." Millie frowned. "Hope the child doesn't have your brain."

"Diablo Seven is a big killer longhorn. He ain't carrying the spirit of a dead man, he's just a mean animal." Sullivan glared at Millie.

"Mama said it's time for me to have a child. Daddy's been trying to find me a feller fer weeks. He looked at all the cowboys around here and the ones bunching that herd a couple weeks ago. Daddy spared your life, he chose you to father my child. You'll live, least till after I give birth to a little one. Then one of us will kill you." She nodded. "Grab some shut-eye, we'll be heading home in a little while." She blew a white powdery substance in his face.

Sullivan inhaled the dust, his eyes rolled back in his head as consciousness left him.

"Briscoe, what took you so long?" Dora jumped from her perch near the cold fire and hurried to his side. Her shout woke Sullivan from a deep sleep.

"Quieten down, Maw," he scolded. "Three cowboys chased Papa off his favorite watering hole. He's bringing them this way."

"See you found this jasper's horse."

"Papa led me to it. It had a thorn deep in the tender of his hoof. Can't carry anybody for a few days but he can drag a sled." He glanced at Sullivan. "You ready to travel?"

"Think so." He nodded.

"See Millie rigged up a drag." Briscoe glanced at his mother. "Is the poultice ready?"

"Finished a little while ago, been letting it cool." She lifted the battered pot and stuck her fingers inside the thick goo.

"Let's get this done and get home." He squatted at Sullivan's side. "This is going to sting a mite. Now you can't yell out or nothing." Dora loosened the bandages, exposing the puckered wound to the open air.

"I'm gonna work this ointment deep into the wound." Briscoe dabbed his fingers in the yellow goo and layered it on Sullivan's punctured flesh.

Waves of intense heat burned through his side, and Sullivan gritted his teeth together, biting back a scream. His lips turned white, sweat beaded on his forehead, his cheeks the color of ripe tomatoes. A muted whine came from his tortured throat. Tears coursed down his cheeks.

"That's good enough; wrap him up and let's get moving." Millie lashed their meager possessions to the makeshift drag.

"I'm gonna load you on the travois." Briscoe bent and cradled the cowboy. He lifted Sullivan from the ground easily and carried him to the drag.

A single black dot appeared before his eyes, he felt dizzy and lightheaded. The whole world seemed to waver and bend at unnatural angles. He closed his eyes, head resting on his saddle, as sleep claimed him.

The sapling frame bounced over the rough ground, and jolted him awake. Pain shot through his side with every bump over the uneven surface. "How much longer do I have to ride in this blasted thing?"

"Be quiet," Millie snapped. "Papa's in that draw yonder. Them cowboys got him all stirred up. Mad as he is, he'll kill us if we ain't careful." She walked by his side, the broken rifle slung over her shoulder.

Briscoe covered the gelding's quivering nostrils. "Those cowboys are gonna try to box him in that draw."

"Stay put." Millie placed the rifle near Sullivan's hands and crept to her brother's side.

"Damned if I will." Sullivan moved his legs to the edge of the travois. He braced the shattered rifle stock on the ground and pushed himself to a standing position. A stabbing pain ran through his side. His clenched teeth sank into his bottom lip, drawing blood. Cold clammy sweat covered his forehead, a lightheaded feeling swept over him. Grim determination forced him to limp forward.

Dora appeared at his side, watching as he limped forward. "Hope my grandchild don't turn out to be as hard-headed as you."

"Ain't gonna be any grandchild."

"We'll see." A gap-toothed smile split her wrinkled face.

"You two hush up," Millie chided.

Three riders raced across a small rise, ropes twirling above their heads. Dust and grass clods flew from shod hooves as they closed on the Longhorn. Seven ran from the draw, and charged the horses.

The bull lowered his head, under the nearest horse, a large bay, fifteen hands high. His wide forehead slammed its broad chest, and flipped the bay over on his back. A wild scream tore from the cowboy's throat as the saddle crushed his ribs. Seven's hoof smashed his skull to bloody shards.

"Damn," Sullivan whispered. "Poor fella didn't have a chance."

Millie's nostrils flared as she spun toward him. "You get that hole to bleeding again, I'll whup you with a Mesquite limb. Mama, take him back to the drag."

"I want to see this." Sullivan leaned on the gelding. "Need to know what I'm up against."

"The only thing yore up against is my sister's good nature," Briscoe mumbled.

Diablo Seven's back feet kicked high in the air. He swiveled on his front feet and charged the second horse and rider. The burly cowboy wheeled the piebald and cast a wide loop at the bull's head. The rope fell over the horns, he jerked a dally around the saddle horn.

Seven's pan sized hooves dug into the dirt. He reached the end of the rope and strained against the braided hemp. He overpowered the piebald and yanked the horse to the ground. The rope popped like a shotgun.

The cowboy rolled to his feet, his left hand grabbing for his pistol. Seven was on him before he cleared leather. The point of the left horn ripped his belly, tearing through his backbone. His scream of agony carried to the hillside. The grinning skull caught on that horn exploded on impact.

The lone survivor spun his mount. He spurred the grullo viciously, as it sprinted for safety. Seven shook his blood stained head and flung the dead cowboy away. The body bounced from the hard dirt and lodged upside down in a scrub oak.

Seven pawed the earth, throwing large clods of dirt on his

back. He jumped forward, breaking into a full run in an instant.

"He'll never make it to the trees." Sullivan shook his head. "Poor bastard's a goner."

"Course he is," Briscoe agreed. "Daddy ain't gonna let him get away."

"You still want to tangle with Seven?" Millie demanded.

"I'm not going to rope him. I'm going to put a fifty caliber bullet in his chest. That'll take the fight out of the biggest animal on the plains." Sullivan clutched at his side.

"Yore a damned idjit. You ain't gonna get a chance to bring Papa down. Yore rifle's busted. Soon as you father my child I'll put a bullet between them blue eyes of yourn." Millie nodded.

"You ain't much for sweet talk are you?" Sullivan licked his dry lips.

Seven closed the distance with the exhausted horse. The cowboy turned his head at the bull's approach, his spurs raked the grullo's bloody hide. The wide eyed animal jumped forward, desperate to reach the safety of the close packed brush. The horse stumbled. The rider flew over the animal's head and smacked the hard earth. The stunned rider rose to his knees. His head swiveled on his shoulders. An ear piercing scream tore from his throat, as Seven's head slammed his back. The force of the blow lifted him into the air, and slammed him to the baked soil. Large hooves crushed his ribs and spine. Seven sniffed the bloody carcass and leisurely walked away, paying little mind to the two horses wandering aimlessly across the small clearing.

"We ain't sparkin'. Yore gonna father my child and then I'm gonna kill you, simple as that." She turned abruptly and walked away.

"Be damned if I will."

"Show's over," Briscoe said. "Get back on the drag. It's time to get home."

"I'm gonna get one of those horses and kill that bull." Sullivan limped to the travois.

"You can't even walk on yore own, how you gonna do

anything?" Millie snapped.

"I'm beginning to think yore daddy could have picked a better man to share yore bed with." Dora shook her head. "It's gonna be a simple-minded, hard-headed child."

"The grullo's not going to make it." Briscoe ran a grimy hand over his whiskered jaw. "Broke the cannon bone most likely, wolves will be eatin' good tonight." His hand closed on the reins.

"I'm gonna kill that bull and carry his head back for the bounty." His eyes hardened to tiny pinpricks of blue. "And I ain't gonna father no child."

"I've got some things back in the cabin that will make you perform." Dora climbed aboard the travois and patted the blanket beside her. "Put a child in her belly and I'll make sure yore days are good ones and you won't suffer none at the end."

"Truthfully, that don't make me feel much better." Sullivan shook his head.

A dull red painted the western sky. They stopped at a small rock and sapling cabin. The sloped roof tapered toward the dirt at a steep angle. Huge stones laid one on top of the other framed the walls. A heavy plank door covered the only entrance.

"It ain't much but it's all they is." Briscoe cleared his throat and spat. "Millie, you and mama, get him in the house. I'll take this knothead down to the corral and doctor that hoof."

Millie turned to Sullivan. "Give me your hand."

"Just hand me my rifle, I'll make it on my own," he insisted.

"Yore a stubborn feller." She passed him the weapon. "After you heal up, I'm gonna come calling."

Sullivan swung his feet to the ground, knuckles whitened around the rifle, as he fought to a standing position. "Made it." His face took on a white pasty color.

"I'll get a fire going under the stew pot." Millie walked by Sullivan's side. "I'll do some hunting tomorrow. Stock up some more food, there'll barely be enough for us tonight."

"We'll fill up on coffee if we have to," Dora's voice carried to their ears.

"Just give me some water." Sullivan clutched at the wall of the hut.

"I hope our kid has yore eyes." Millie nodded. "I want a blue-eyed child."

"There ain't gonna be any child."

"I've seen men stand in line to spend a few minutes with a woman, and plant their seed in her body." Dora glared at Sullivan. "Millie is offering herself to you, all you have to do is perform."

"It's different when I pay for a woman. I don't expect her to kill me when it's over."

"My grandchild's gonna be loved, it'll have a family, a mama, Grandma, and uncle, a family."

"What about the father?" Sullivan nodded.

"We'll tell stories about what a good man you was." Millie grinned. "Now get in there."

Sullivan woke late the next morning. His empty belly growled. A chill shook his sweat-soaked body. Flies buzzed around the bloody shirt wrapped around his middle. He wanted to scratch but pushed the notion from his mind. Dried blood flaked away from the shirt as he peeled the makeshift bandage back to examine the wound. Dark yellow ooze formed in the center and drained toward his spine.

"What the hell are you doing?" Briscoe shouted. "Get back in bed. Millie went after some herbs and roots that should help that wound heal."

"Damn thing's trying to get infected. And I'm chilling." Sullivan's teeth clattered together.

"Figured that'd happen." Briscoe threw a ratty quilt on the bed. "That'll keep you warm." He nodded toward the coffee pot. "Want to sip on some brew?"

"I reckon." Sullivan decided the need for warmth overruled

the coffee's foul taste.

"While yore drinking that, I'll cook us some vittles." Briscoe smacked his lips.

"What are we having?" A frown touched Sullivan's face as he sipped the coffee.

"Got some meat, all I could carry." Briscoe placed a bulky hide wrapped bundle on the table.

Sullivan noticed the mouse colored hair and knew Briscoe had found the grullo. The foul brew soured on his stomach. "Was it dead?"

"No." He shook his head. "It was suffering something awful, had to put it down. Figure I got fifty or sixty pounds of meat there, chest and hindquarter. After I cook us up a meal, I'll smoke the rest."

"Never developed a taste for horse meat." Sullivan shook his head.

"We don't let anything go to waste out here. We eat whatever we can and we're damned grateful to get it." Briscoe unwrapped his prize. He added small sticks to the embers in the crude fireplace. When it was burning to his satisfaction, he hung the meat on wood spits and let the fat drip into the flames.

Heat quickly filled the small cabin. Sullivan kicked the covers from his body, his hair and chest soaked with sweat. The odor of roasting meat made his stomach roll.

"I want to surprise mama. We haven't had good meat in two weeks." Briscoe nodded.

The steady drum of pounding hooves drifted to Sullivan's ears.

"Someone's coming," he mumbled. "Riding awful hard."

"Got to be Millie." Briscoe stepped to the door. "Did you find the herbs and things?"

"Where's Mama?" Millie exhaled a deep breath, her face red and sweaty. "Seven went to the salt lick to check on his brood cows. One or two were in season and needed attention. Managed to catch this piebald and gather the weapons off the dead fellers. Found some good roots and herbs down near the clayside."

"Maw's tending her onion garden," Briscoe said. "Good thing you found that stuff. His gut's starting to swell."

"Damn it." The smile vanished from her face. "He's not gonna die. I'll see to that. He's got a child to father."

"I think you should kill this un and find another fella. This un's gonna be trouble."

Millie glared at her brother. "I ain't gonna get sweet on him. I'll have him up on his feet in a week. I figure I can be with child inside of two weeks." She untied the saddle bags and yanked them free. "Especially with mama's potions."

"I won't share a bed with you." Sullivan staggered to the door, the quilt draped over his shoulders.

"You'll do what I want when the time comes," Millie snapped. "Get on the bed. I need to look at that hole."

"I won't do it." He crept to the bed and sat down.

"Shut up." She slapped him across the face. He flopped to his back as she yanked the crusty bandage from his side. "I'm getting tired of yore sass. Good thing I got the herbs. You'd be draining pus tomorrow. Be dead within a week."

"Need some help?" Dora hobbled through the door, two large onions gripped in her fist.

Millie nodded. "Boil these roots down, I'm gonna grind these leaves to powder." She glanced at her mother, and pulled a Le Mat pistol from her waist. "Found this on one of them cowboys. It's loaded. If he tries anything, put a round in his leg."

"My pleasure," Dora cackled.

"I'm gonna be gone a few days. When I come back you better be ready to perform."

"Where are you going?" Sullivan demanded.

"Coolwater Creek, take me a bath." She hesitated by the door. "Chain him to the big post down at the corral. Doctor him every day and make sure he eats. I don't want him to have any excuses when I get back."

Dora centered the Le Mat on Sullivan's chest. "You done pissed her off." Her wide smile displayed her single remaining tooth.

"Go on, eat yore fill." She glanced toward the door. "Briscoe, after we doctor on Orange, he goes to the corral."

"Shore nuff, Mama. Be ready in a minute."

Sullivan brushed a buzzing fly away from his face. The aroma of fresh cooked meat slowly filled his nostrils and drove sleep away. He opened his eyes to see the plate of food and a hot cup of coffee sitting on the ground within his reach.

The chain around his ankle jangled as he crawled across rocky ground to the waiting food. He grabbed the cup and slurped the hot liquid. He ignored the harsh taste of ground mesquite seeds. He closed his eyes and swallowed. His dirty fingers circled the horse steak and flat bread. Grease dripped from his fingers as he bit the thick steak.

"No need to wolf it down like that." Briscoe sat on his haunches, just out of Sullivan's reach. "There's more food if yore still hungry."

Sullivan wiped his chin, his eyes fastened on Briscoe and Dora. "She's coming back, ain't she?"

"Be here tonight," Dora cackled. "Wants you cleaned up and ready for sparkin." She waved the pistol at the lock holding the chain around the post. "Stay put now, Briscoe's gonna get you loose. Don't try nothing, I'll put a bullet in yore foot, should you try."

"Just put a bullet in me now." Sullivan rattled the chain locked around his ankle. "Soon as I get a chance, I'm gonna get loose."

"Time you spent out here ain't mellowed you a lick." Briscoe freed the chain from the post. He stuffed the lock and key into his vest pocket. "Gather up that chain, you ain't gonna run very fast packing that."

"Where are we going?" Sullivan drained the coffee and tossed the cup to the ground. He stepped forward gingerly, holding the chain in one hand and the horse meat in the other.

"Down to the pool. Yore gonna scrub up and shave." Dora

motioned with the pistol. "Just keep going that way, you can't miss it."

The brown grass poked at Sullivan's bare feet, after a hundred yards small bits of gravel and pebbles covered the path. He spied a glint of sunlight on water ahead. Large rocks surrounded the pool on three sides. A sand and gravel bank sloped gently to the water.

"Get in." Briscoe ordered. "I've got some clean clothes for you on those rocks yonder when yore finished."

"It'd be easier without this chain." Sullivan jingled the links together.

"Just do what yore told." Dora smacked her lips. "When Millie gets done with you, I might have a go myself before we kill you."

"Here you go." Briscoe tossed a slab into the water. "That's some good lye soap, made from horse fat and ashes. Lather up real good."

Sullivan grabbed the bar before it sank to the bottom, he waded to the middle of the pool and dropped the chain. The water lapped at his waist, he closed his eyes and sank below the mirror-like surface.

The ripples spread to the far banks before Sullivan popped into the air, water streaming from his hair and beard. He scrubbed the soap along his chest and arms. "Where's Millie?"

"She's close by, making herself pretty." Dora grinned. "Don't forget to warsh your hair."

"I imagine Diablo Seven is with her?" The lye soap made thick lather in his greasy hair.

"Yeah, he's there." Briscoe nodded. "Here's your shaving tools." He laid a straight razor and a small mirror on the bank.

Sullivan sank beneath the water and rinsed the soap from his body. He waded to the bank and grabbed the razor. "What, no hot water?"

"Do the best you can." Briscoe backed away.

Sullivan lathered his beard with the lye soap, holding the mirror in his left hand he began to shave with his right. "You put a good edge on this razor, nice and sharp."

"Papa taught us the proper way to sharpen a blade." Briscoe nodded.

Sullivan ran the edge across his forearm, the sharp steel cut into his flesh. "Damn, that is sharp, didn't need any pressure at all."

"What the hell are you doing?" Dora jumped to her feet. "Put that down right now. Do what I said." The pistol trembled in her hand.

"You ain't gonna kill me." Sullivan grinned. "But I can slice my wrists and bleed out quick in this water." He dropped the arm under the surface, a pink stain circled his waist.

"Briscoe, get in there and stop him."

Her son dropped his gunbelt to the ground and waded into the pool. "Give me that razor."

"I'll give you a little bit of it." Sullivan held his right hand away from his side, water dripping from the sharp edge. "You can't out and out kill me, not with me being the chosen one to mate with your sister." He slashed at Briscoe's face.

Briscoe ducked under his hand and lunged through the water, his arms circling Sullivan's waist. He lifted Sullivan in the air, and slammed him into the water. They broke the surface moments later, the chain gripped in Sullivan's hands wrapped tightly around Briscoe's throat.

"Get off him." Dora waded toward them, the Le Mat pointed at Sullivan's chest. "Get off my son."

Sullivan dropped the chain and lashed out with the razor, the blade slicing across the back of Dora's empty hand. She jumped back, her blood mixing with the expanding crimson stain.

Briscoe grabbed Sullivan's hands and rose to his feet. He flipped the man over his head toward the bank. The chain caught around Briscoe's throat and forced him down.

Sullivan's feet slammed Dora's head, the old woman dropped to her knees. The pistol flew from her hands, landing near the water's edge. Her hands fisted in Sullivan's hair, holding his face under the water. Sullivan lashed out blindly, the razor cut deeply into yielding flesh. He stumbled to his feet, flinging water from his eyes.

Dora lay on her back, her hands wrapped around her throat, trying to stop the jet of blood shooting from her jugular. Sullivan waded toward the bank, the chain tightened around his ankle dragging him back. He glanced over his shoulder.

"You killed mama," Briscoe screamed, his hands wrapped around the chain, pulling Sullivan toward the deeper water. "I'm gonna make you suffer, Orange."

Dora, in her death throes, kicked the razor from his hand. Sullivan spied the pistol lying on the bank. He leaped forward, pawing at the grip.

"No, you don't." Briscoe splashed forward. "When Millie's done with you, I'm gonna kill you slow."

"Hold him, Briscoe. Don't let him get away." Millie and Diablo Seven appeared on the path.

Sullivan felt a moment's slack in the chain as Briscoe glanced at his sister. His fingers curled around the pistol grip as the tension on the chain returned. He turned, finger on the trigger. He thumb cocked the hammer and fired, the pistol bucked in his hand.

Briscoe's mouth dropped open in surprise, the chain slipped from his grasp. A red flower blossomed on his chest as he sank to his knees. "Should have killed you the day we found you," he mumbled.

The rumble of cloven hooves on rock echoed behind him, small pebbles splashed near his feet. Sullivan wheeled, his thumb found the hammer. He centered the sights on Seven's shoulders and pulled the trigger. Fire spit from the end of the barrel.

Diablo Seven stumbled, he recovered his balance quickly and kept running. Millie jumped from the path and disappeared into the undergrowth. Sullivan wiped wet hair from his eyes as he cocked the hammer a third time. He centered the sights on the bull's forehead and squeezed the trigger gently. Sullivan scarcely noticed the recoil.

Diablo Seven's front legs buckled, he collapsed, his nose plowed through the sand and gravel. The bull slid to a halt, his head submerged in the pool. Air bubbles broke the surface above his nostrils.

"You killed my whole family," Millie shouted. "But you ain't gonna cut daddy's head off and turn it in for bounty."

Sullivan stared at the brush and rocks, trying in vain to locate Millie's position. "I ain't gonna try, all I want to do now is get out of here alive."

"Take what you need and git. But know this, you won't ever know happiness. Every woman, everyone you care about will come to a bad end. And when it's yore time, our son will be there to kill you."

"We ain't been together. We ain't gonna have a kid." Sullivan tugged on the chain, pulling Briscoe's body closer. He searched the body and found the key at the end of a rawhide string tied around the dead man's neck. The lock at his ankle opened easily. "Don't come after me, Millie. I'll kill you if I ever see you again." He raced up the hill, unmindful of the pebbles and rough grass tearing at his feet.

"I'll have my way with you, Orange. Sooner than you think. I'll have my way with you."

Sullivan pawed at his face, shielding his eyes from the mid-day sun directly over his head. He glanced at his campfire, the ashes were gray and cold. His head felt thick and fuzzy. "What the hell happened to me?" He tried to gain his feet and noticed his pants were down at his ankles.

Sullivan focused on his busted Springfield rifle sitting on the ground neat the coffee pot. He stumbled to his feet, a vague memory surfacing in his mind. He dreamed of Jocelyn. She had appeared in camp in the middle of the night. He drew the Le Mat, but couldn't squeeze the trigger. As Jocelyn stepped closer, her face reshaped itself to Millie's.

She blew a handful of dust in his face and they made love under the stars. Sullivan buttoned his pants. He quickly packed his belongings and saddled the horse he'd taken from Millie's home. He climbed aboard the animal and lit out, ever conscious of her eyes staring at him from a distance.

"I'm carrying yore son, Orange. He'll find you when it's yore time." Her voice carried on the light wind. "He'll find you."

SIEGE

by Mike Loniewski

When I was a child there was talk of wild men, savages poisoning the land and spreading disease like rabid wolves. We'd gotten word from riders, recounting tales of the settlements they'd passed through.

"They had a taste for flesh," one rider said.

If my brother and I showed any signs of terror from these stories father would make us pay the price for it. He expected more from us, even as children. Father preached that the difference between men of cowardice and men of bravery was that the former succumbed to fear, the latter simply had no time for it.

The stories grew more frequent and soon a group of settlers had come to convince my father to take up arms with them. I remember hearing the large men argue with him through the walls of our modest home. They insisted that strength was in numbers and that we'd never survive the sickness on our own. Father respectfully disagreed, said "If the end is near I'll face it in the comfort of my own home."

They mocked him, calling him names that would make a lesser man lash out. I always wondered why father didn't batter these men like they deserved. My father been a soldier. He'd killed braver men than these bloated pig farmers, killed them with his bare hands in the great charges of the Civil War. Years later, I came to understand his reasons. Father was simply the better man, fearless and confident. He never wavered in his character, even on that day when the rotted man appeared in the distance.

This disease-ridden man crested the horizon, stumbling from exhaustion and horrid wounds. His clothes were in tatters, caked with a muddied blood. I felt fear creeping in at the sight of him. I thought of my father's words and struggled to bury that fear deep inside. I would not let him see it across my face.

Father remained calm, mounting his horse and instructing us to tell mother that he was going to see about a man on our property and that she was to have provisions ready when he returned.

My younger brother Vern and I hurried to our mother and did our best to explain our father's wishes. As she tended to them, we hustled to the weathered wooden fence that enclosed our hogs. The fence was high and sturdy, the perfect vantage point to take in our father's bravery. We climbed up, our muddied shoes slipping on the wood. Vern needed help, of course.

I had managed to grab my father's rifle scope as we rushed out the door. Balancing myself on the top board, I pulled on the lens, elongating it, and raised it to my eye. The plain seemed to bend through the fish-eyed lens. I dragged the scope across the horizon, searching until I found my father.

He was careful on his approach. Father had tended to trespassers on our land before and knew quite well what precautions to take. He circled the man at first, surveying his condition from a distance. He then scanned the horizon, checking for trackers or a swarm of bandits on the stranger's trail.

My vantage point didn't sit well with Vern in the slightest. Through nagging tugs I struggled to keep the scope to my eye. The tugging and whining grew incessant and it became too much of a hassle to fend him off. Little brothers are known for their cunning strategies of annoyance, and Vern was a master of the art. I surrendered the scope and climbed down into the mud-caked pen. I began to think of the stories, the ones from the riders. I thought of what these wild men would have looked like, eating the skin of some besieged settler. My mind was filled with gruesome images, adding to a fear that was growing more intense.

Vern's shouting snapped me back to our situation at the fence. He was blabbering about father and his Colt revolver, the one he'd used on the battlefields against Confederate assassins. I climbed back up the rickety boards and wrestled the scope from his hands.

When I found him on the horizon, father had dismounted and was holding a handkerchief to his face. He was aiming his revolver, leveling it toward the stranger. I could see him clearly now, this rotted man. He was covered with jagged gashes that oozed an inky, black blood. His face was smeared with an oily sludge, his eyes hollow. He had fallen to his knees now, his head slung forward, swaying back and forth hypnotically.

I moved the scope back to my father. He was saying something to the man, shouting to him. The man lunged. There was a struggle, I could barely manage to keep the scope to my eyes. My father fought himself free from his grip and stepped back. Then he cocked his revolver and the hammer dropped.

The sound of the gunshot ripped across the plain like a clap of thunder. It nearly knocked Vern and me off the fence. I steadied myself and searched through the scope to find them. The rotted man lay in heap, gun smoke rising from his head.

I'd imagined my father on the battlefield many times before, bayonetting his enemies, pulling off crack shots as a sniper. It was glamorous in my mind. This was anything but. He killed a man and left his corpse to rot. This was what killing a man looked like. My hands started to tremble, the scope rattling.

Father returned in a fierce gallop. When he dismounted, he rushed past us, carrying with him an awful stench. It was a heavy, rotted smell that hung inside my nose. He was clutching his hand, a look of discomfort on his face. There was concern to him that I'd never seen before and, admittedly, I was frightened by it. Mother was waiting at the door. She took one look at his hand. Blood was running from it. Father ushered her inside and shut the door.

Vern and I rushed to the house and squatted down beneath a window, cupping our ears for the muffled sounds inside. I heard words like rabid and fever, and the name Huddleston.

The Huddleston farm was much like ours in that it consisted of a single family. Their children, four of them, were all older than Vern and myself. I had met their father when we gathered together for a meal one winter. He was thin, much like the rotted man on the horizon. If the stranger was Mr. Huddleston, he was attacked with such savagery that it left him unrecognizable.

Father emerged from the door, his hand bandaged and a soldier's purpose burning in his eyes. With a stern voice he ordered us to lock up the livestock and meet him 'round back.

My father had a rule that was more of an enforced law. He expected us to be good soldiers, to trust his decisions and go forth with them. Questions, then, were not something he wanted to hear. With Vern rattling them off one after another, I was beginning to worry more about him catching a whooping from father than I was about the rotted man. I dragged him off before his backside met my father's wrath.

When we reached the pen only one hog had managed to wander off. Our hogs were renowned for their laziness. I attempted to coax it back to the pen before it suddenly stopped at the gate. A few nudges at the hind quarters and the darned thing waddled on into the pen, mocking me with a few snorts. Above it all, Vern never stopped his list of questions. I yelled at him to quit asking and to latch the gate.

When we returned to the house father was lugging heavy burlap sacks over his shoulder. He was covered in sweat, carrying a bunch of shovels under his arm. He threw them down at our feet and rubbed the soreness from his shoulders and neck. He ordered us to grab a shovel and fill the sacks with as much dirt as they could hold.

We worked fast and soon had a large pile of sacks packed tightly. Father was on the flat dirt roof as he pulled them up to his perch. We did our best to help, but the bags were heavy. I could tell that he was setting them up strategically. They were defenses. For what, I could not be sure.

A few bags were left and he told us to take them inside and stack them by the door and windows. We sured up the defenses inside the best we could and then headed out on back.

Father was waiting for us with the rifles. It was clear that something was coming. We had always heard the dreaded stories of vengeful Sioux warriors slaughtering unsuspecting settlers. I wasn't ready for it, and I was just as scared of our fate as I was of failing my father.

We were no strangers to firearms, only now we were going to use them for something other than shooting livestock. After watching my father kill earlier, I wasn't sure I had the stomach for it. Father pulled us close as he loaded his carbine. He seemed distant, like he'd just awoken from a horrible sleep. He'd grown pale and spoke slowly.

"Do you remember what I told you boys? Just one shot at a time and don't let your nerves get the best of you. Breathe out when you pull the trigger."

Vern was panicking. He started asking questions, brimming with tears. Father pulled him closer. Calmly, he told Vern to take his rifle inside and to stay by mother's side and then pushed him toward the door. He then turned to me and ordered me to grab two rifles. We were heading to the roof.

He set me up behind a stack of bags to his right. We knelt together as he checked his rifles one last time, the bandage on his hand soaked through with a deep, oily red. I could feel the roof beginning to shake and I realized it was not from us. The ground itself was rumbling, a constant, deep vibration growing stronger. Riders were approaching.

Father leaned in close, the sweat soaking his body. There was a smell to him. His eyes were hollow and he spoke drowsily. I remember his words well.

"You don't get frightened, James. You don't get frightened

because I've prepared you. I want you to be prepared for what you'll have to do. You have every right to be scared of what you'll see. But you won't be scared, will you, James?"

I didn't know what he meant. I choked out an answer anyway.

"Mr. Huddleston, he needed me. I wasn't ready. But not my son. My son is prepared."

There was a wheeze to his breath, a sour smell seeping from his pores.

"When it happens, you don't wait. I'll fight as long as I can but when it happens, you'll have to do it. You close your eyes and you do it. You won't be scared."

I was confused. I froze, terrified by the rumbling, the smell, and my father's sickness.

He pulled me at the collar, impatient. The rumbling was enough to drive you mad. He spoke one last time before the horde came into view.

"You won't be scared. Say it back to me."

I answered.

The riders rose up from the horizon, filling the line between earth and heaven. They were formless at first, like black ink etched across the land. As they barreled toward us, their form became more distinct. They weren't Sioux.

Upon rotted horses rode withered, putrid corpses. Their flesh was like blackened leather, stretched thin over crooked bone. They were wraiths, riding from the gates of hell to claim our souls.

The smell started to move in, that same rotted smell that followed my father. Father steadied me and gave the orders. He told me to single out a rider to my right. I aimed at the center of its chest. It was hollow. A jagged wound exposed gray bone within the cavity. I aimed higher. The head was intact and I decided that was where I would shoot.

He reminded me to breathe out once more. I exhaled and pulled the trigger toward me. The rifle kicked into my shoulder and I watched the rider's head shatter in a cloud of black ink and grey bone. I reloaded quickly, the shaking in my hands beginning to steady.

Father had begun his assault as well, each of us sending a volley of fire over the roof. We were swarmed now, father yelling over the thundering stampede of undead, reminding me to pick one target at a time. I unloaded my rifle, each shot seeming to hit its mark. I turned to father, looking for my second rifle.

I heard something rip past my ear. A zip like the beating wings of a passing dragonfly. I heard the zip again. An arrow, withered and old, had embedded into the bag in front of me. A hail of three or four more and I fell to the floor in fear. Father yelled for me to reload and fire back. When I peered back up we had been engulfed by hell itself.

Surrounded on all sides, father ordered me to concentrate my fire on the front of our home. He moved positions to cover our rear, dodging arrows as he went. I could hear mother yelling to us from below. I couldn't answer. My throat had seized up and I threw all of my efforts into firing my rifle. Then the bullets came up from underneath us.

They came in a quick succession, ripping up from the center of the roof and splintering wood. Mother's screams were clear now. Something was inside. That's when the fever took hold of my father.

He had stumbled over the bags, seizing and vomiting. The bile spewed uncontrollably, foul and putrid. My father folded from the pressure inside of him. I ran to him, trying to pull him to his feet. He pushed me away forcefully, shouting for me to get the rifle. He turned to look at me. His eyes were fading, turning a hollow, milky white. The vomit that stained his chin was black as pitch. He shouted again and again, pleading for me to get the rifle. He was fighting something inside him, a demon seeping into his veins. He began to shake wildly, choking on his own tongue, a wet rattle coming from his chest.

The body that stood before me was no longer my father.

It looked at me with pale, gray skin, stained and putrid. It lunged for me, ravenous with hunger. I panicked and dropped my rifle and stumbled over the bags. I scrambled on all fours, trying to create space between myself and this rotted man. There was the sound of wood snapping beneath me. In an instant, the roof gave way.

My legs dangled through the jagged hole, my arms struggling to keep me on the roof, my fingers clawing into the splintered wood. I felt a pull on my ankles. I looked down and saw a corpse's hand wrapped around my leg, its boney fingers twisting tighter like knotted vines. There was fresh blood slathered over its body. Fresh blood. My mother and brother's.

I kicked and kicked, trying to work my legs free. Then sharp pain on top of my head. My father had grabbed a fistful of my hair and I was pulled violently in both directions. I felt snapping below me, not of my bones, but of the corpse's, its arms splitting from its body like dried meat. I was pulled up by my hair, pulled face to face with my father.

The smell was awful. His mouth widened, releasing a deeper odor of rancid death. I pulled away, fighting against him, punching his chest, his throat. I pulled down hard, away from his face, struggling to break free from his grip. I was pressed against his body. It was damp and cold and foul. The holster on his waist hit me in my head.

My father's Colt revolver. It still hung in the holster, loaded and ready to fire. I reached and grabbed for it. The heavy gun was in my hands now. I pulled the hammer back, just like my father had shown me so many times before. I fired. The blast from the gun punched back into my hands.

Again, I cocked the hammer and pulled the trigger. There was space between us now. He lunged back toward me. I closed my eyes and aimed high. The revolver kicked and I felt the wet spray across my face. A mushy hole sat atop my father's head, and he collapsed lifelessly to the floor.

Heads of the undead began to come into view all around me, their only sound was a raspy, rattling breath. I held the revolver, smoking in my hands. It was empty. The firing had stopped. It was silent now. I closed my eyes tightly, and called for my father to save me one last time. Then there was thunder.

Loud, powerful rounds slammed into the side of the house. A repetitive, loud clanking of metal accompanied the splintering of wood, the shattering of bone, the tearing of flesh. Something was firing in the distance. I dove out of harm's way. The onslaught of projectiles only increased, coming from all angles.

I watched from the floor as the corpses were turned into a black mist, torn apart by the unseen ordinance. I could hear horses, live horses, not the dead carcasses that rode into battle. And there were the sounds of men charging toward me. A great, booming voice in the distance ordered a cease fire. I laid still, my hands moving down away from my ears. There was a creaking of wood and I could feel the weight of someone on the roof.

My rescuer was a member of the Seventh Cavalry. He grabbed me without saying a word and lowered me down to the waiting arms of his fellow soldiers. Scattered rifle shots rang out as one soldier gave me a looking over. He commented on the black blood on my face. He shook me, asking me if it had gotten in my mouth or my eyes. I couldn't answer. A commanding officer put his hand on the soldier and ordered him to clean me up.

As they continued to poke and prod I sank deeper into shock, a disconnected sensation that emanated from the pit of my bowels and coursed through every limb.

I heard them. A pair of soldiers exiting the house. In a manner most cold, they announced the discovery of my family's remains. The commanding officer then ordered the property set ablaze along with all bodies. It was a finality that my young soul was unprepared for.

I was carried out on horseback, and as we rode westward I turned back only once to see the thick, black smoke rising skyward. The entirety of my life, all that had ever loved me, burned within the blistering embers. I closed my eyes and didn't open them again until we reached the supply lines.

The plague faded as swiftly as it had struck, an inexplicably cruel force of nature that left those alive pleading to God for answers. Those answers never came. I spent years battling the nightmares and reliving the day my family was taken. The fear crippled me, until father's words echoed in my memory and shook me to my feet. I've grown older now. I've a family of my own, two sons who look to me for the guidance of a father. The fear has been pushed down, away from the surface of my mind. I've no time for it.

THE SHOWGiRL AND THE WENDiGO

by Milo James Fowler

The town of Green Valley stretched out like a great, big bear rug between the hills of northern Texas, land that had long been little more than cattle country. Many a bloody battle between sheepherders and ranchers was fought over this precious soil where the grass sprouted forth so readily. But decades had passed; the sheepherders were driven off, and what remained of the cattlemen wasn't much to speak of. One ranch survived—the Double J, located ten miles north of town—the only link left to remind folks what anchored Green Valley to this land.

Lonnie Lane, a vivacious struggling actress hailing from eastern Pennsylvania, arrived in town on the noon train. She was in her mid-twenties, ivory-skinned, with hair that shone like fresh copper. Her relatives had insisted her trip to Texas was a mistake. Too young, they said she was, for the rough Western life. She would burn terribly under the hot Texas sun. She had her whole life ahead of her—why not bide her time and marry a good Pennsylvanian man? Why chase after a foolish dream?

She stood on the train station platform, searching the bobbing heads in the tide of passengers. According to her benefactor's letter, he was the owner of the largest theater in Green Valley and in desperate need of a girl with a new face. He'd seen her picture in the newspaper and had paid her way to travel west with the promise of a lead in his latest production.

She was accustomed to catching the eyes of passersby, but the gaping expressions on the townsfolk became a bit unsettling. Perhaps they had never seen a well-dressed lady before. Careful to keep the shade of her parasol between her and the scorching sun, she looked to and fro until she noticed a large black man waving to her. She couldn't be sure at first that his gestures were meant for her, but then he called out in a southern drawl.

"Miz Lane! You Miz Lane?"

Lonnie smiled and navigated her way through the crowd to where he stood, hat in hand with large white teeth and age-yellowed eyes. He bent forward at the shoulders and waist to make up for their difference in height.

"I knowed it was you, soon as I seen you." His short, grizzled beard and hair were a sharp contrast against his skin tone. He took Lonnie's hand in his pair, dwarfing it between his callused palms. "Mo, I says, now there's that pretty Pennsylvania gal the boss done hired for his new show!"

Lonnie blushed in spite of herself. "Mr. Irving sent you?"

"Yes, ma'am, Moses Gray's my name proper, and I'm here to escort you to Mr. Irving straight away. Got the buckboard hitched and ready to go."

Squeezing her hand kindly, he led her out through the throngs, who cleared a path like villagers scurrying to keep out from under a giant's foot. Her only luggage consisted of a single steamer trunk and the valise she kept with her at all times. Mo hefted the trunk onto his broad shoulders and slid it into the back of the buckboard. He helped her up to her seat behind the chestnut mare and joined her. Then with a snap of the reins, they were off.

It wasn't long before they arrived at a huge false front with GREEN VALLEY THEATRE painted in bright red on white. HOME OF THE GORGEOUS GLAMOUR GALS, THE GOLDEN SUNSETS! But the doors were closed, and the place looked vacant.

"Just the time of day is all," Mo assured her. "Come nightfall, this is the hottest spot in town."

Lonnie gasped. "Is that—?" She pointed at what looked to be the remains of a small naked child lying outside the backstage door. There were no features she recognized, only pink mutilated flesh and blood—lots of it.

"That shouldn't be there." Wiping at his mouth self-consciously, Mo climbed down from the buckboard and looped the horse's reins over a hitching rail. With quick strides, he came to the corpse and reached for its hind leg. "Just one of the pigs, Miz Lane. Somethin' must've gotten to it. Coyotes, I reckon."

"I see." She averted her eyes and focused on breathing.

Shaking his head, Mo returned to take her trunk from the rear of the buckboard and heft it onto his thick-muscled shoulder. He glanced at Lonnie with a bashful smile as he helped her down from her seat. Then without another word, he led her inside.

"Well, Miss Lane, what do you make of our little town?" Mr. William Irving, owner and manager of Green Valley's most popular theater, sat behind a massive desk in his plush office. He wore a tailored wool suit that stretched about his muscular arms and shoulders. "Not so grand as your eastern cities, I'm sure, but we'll get there. We're moving up in the world."

Lonnie sat across from him in a slat-backed chair and studied the man, trying to decide what sort of manager he would be. She'd left the best director she'd ever worked with back home. It wasn't the pay that had drawn her to Texas, even though Mr. Irving promised her more than twice what she'd ever earned before. It was the prestige she knew her talents deserved.

"I'm impressed, Mr. Irving. Honestly, I didn't know quite what to expect—"

"Call me William, and I'll call you Lonnie. Do we have a deal?"

"Very well." She dipped her chin with a smile.

"I'll bet there are plenty of trashy dime novels circulating about our great state—not that you would read any of that garbage. It taints an Easterner's view of the West—Texas, in particular.

We are, after all, an unincorporated republic, populated with all manner of uncivilized ruffians."

Irving winked at her and stood. A stocky man with the build of a wrestler, he walked with a slight limp, favoring his left leg. An array of liquor bottles sat on a polished table, and he poured a pair of tumblers, holding out one of the glasses to Lonnie as he returned to his desk. "Time to celebrate," he said with a broad smile.

"But Mr.—*William*, I don't even know what my role—"

"A toast." Teeth gleaming unnaturally in the lamplight, he raised his glass and waited for her to do the same. "To new opportunities."

Coyote Cal and Big Yap were in need of work, plain and simple. They didn't have a single copper cent between them. The ranches they'd passed on their journey from Arroyo Seco had been few and far between, and they'd been met with the same response at every turn: "No need for new hands, but try the Double J in Green Valley."

"Which is good news in a way, Cal. If they'd needed *hands*, they would've been plum outta luck with us. We ain't surgeons!" Big Yap guffawed at his own joke—nearly losing his false teeth in the process—seeming to think it was the most hilarious thing he'd heard in quite a spell. But he soon noticed Cal didn't agree. The lean young man rode without a word, eyeing the desolate terrain around them. It was going to be a cold winter in Texas, and the plains appeared to have already gone into hibernation. "Whatcha pondering, Cal?"

He stirred from his reverie and glanced at his sidekick. "Life. Death. Everything in between, I guess."

"So…nothing important?" Yap winked. Over the past few years since he'd started riding with Calvin, it was clear the fellow carried a burden—a darkness that loomed beyond his reach. He'd been just a kid when they first met, and he wasn't much older now—all of eighteen years upon the earth. Young people needed to smile. So it fell to Big Yap to cheer him up. "You know, I've been thinking, too. If there ain't honest work to be had ranchin' and whatnot, what would you think of doing a little bounty huntin'? That way, we'd at least get *paid* for bein' heroes! You know how many times we've brought criminals to justice without accepting the reward?"

"Haven't kept count, Yap."

"Well, I have, and it's been closer to twenty than not. Can you imagine? We'd be livin' high on the hog iffin we had all that reward money in our saddlebags!"

Cal shook his head. "We just try to do what's right. We don't expect anything in return."

"Justice being its own reward or some such?"

"Something like that."

The sound of galloping hoof beats punctuated the distance as a rider approached as fast as his horse could carry him. Cal and Yap drew rein.

"He's killin' that dang critter!" Big Yap observed.

The rider spotted Coyote Cal and Big Yap ahead of him and jerked his reins, digging in with his heels and forcing his mount off the trail into the brush—suspicious behavior, to say the least. Cal kicked his horse into a gallop that would easily overtake the rider. Such was the mount our young hero rode: the mighty palomino, Thunder. Big Yap struggled to keep up on his paint mare, Blossom, but within seconds, they'd closed in on the racing stranger and flanked him. Over the wild, thudding rhythm of their horses' hoof beats, Cal ordered the large man to pull up. The rider jerked his head sideways to cast a feverish glance at Cal, then screamed something unintelligible and aimed the pistol in his grip. The shot was wild, hot lead whizzing past Cal's ear. Ducking, our hero drew his Colt in a flash and fired it into the air.

"Pull up!" he shouted.

At the same time, Big Yap leaped from his saddle and tackled the rider, dropping him from his horse. They hit the ground hard, and the stranger gave Yap a kick that sent him sprawling across the dust. The wiry sidekick was up on his feet in an instant, whipping out the sawed-off shotgun from the scabbard on his back.

"You wanna play rough?" He leveled both barrels on the stranger. "Reach!"

"Don't you shoot, please don't." The man held up his hands in surrender, his bloodshot eyes glassy with tears. Judging by the grey in his whiskers, he and Yap were about the same age—past half a century.

The stranger dropped to his knees, his shoulders quaking. "She was so young." His voice became a mournful baritone. "I shoulda known somethin' was wrong, but I didn't do *nothin'*!" He covered his face and trembled.

"What's his problem?" Yap squinted at Cal.

"Go round up his horse."

Cal approached the kneeling man. Big Yap didn't stir; as always, his curiosity was stronger than a feline's. But he sent Blossom after the man's mount.

"I was just doin' my job, picked her up at the depot, but I shoulda *known*—"

"Speak sense," Cal said. "Who are you running from?"

The man wiped his face on his sleeve and stood, more than six and a half feet of him and close to three hundred pounds of muscle. Tears clung to his eyes. "You ain't been sent after me?"

Cal and Yap glanced at each other, then shook their heads.

With a short sigh, the man said, "Name's Moses Gray. I work for Mister William Irving, owner of the Green Valley Theater..."

In the manager's office, Mr. William Irving stood with a bandaged forearm as he talked to the town's greenhorn of a sheriff, one Clint Morgan.

"So you say that Negro's worked for you how long now?"

"I understand you're new to this territory, son, but the man has a name, and it's *Moses*. He's been in my employ for close to a decade, I reckon—ever since I opened the theater. A good man, one I could trust." His expression darkened. "Never figured him to be a killer. He was a gentle giant—ask anyone in town!"

"I aim to."

Irving shook his head. "Come to think of it though, I should've known when I saw the look in his eyes…"

"How's that?" Morgan shifted his weight from one foot to the other with a wince.

"Noticed it right off, I'm afraid, but I didn't think anything of it: the way he kept looking at that poor girl—*shameful*. The way men on the prowl will look a woman over like she's fresh meat. I should have reprimanded him, of course, but I let it go. He always struck me as the harmless type."

Morgan cleared his throat. "So, last night—"

"Miss Lane screamed." Irving limped to his liquor table. "I could hear her clearly: 'Get away from me!' she cried. Her voice came from backstage, and I hastened there as fast as I could— bum leg and all." He punched his left leg with a fist. "Mo came at me with a knife. I got out of his way, but he managed to cut me as he ran past." He lifted his bandaged arm. "When I found Miss Lane on the floor in the dark, she was…as you've already seen." It was improper to dwell upon the gory details of the poor girl's ordeal. "I sent one of my employees after the doctor, but it was too late for him to be of any earthly good."

With a heavy sigh, Irving collapsed into his desk chair and sipped at his tumbler of brandy. "I don't know how I'm going to write her parents. I sent for her, you see, from Pennsylvania, promising her a lead in my follies—a Golden Sunset to remember."

Sheriff Morgan nodded. "Green Valley isn't the sort of town where showgirls end up stabbed to death, Mr. Irving. It's rather an open-and-shut case, the way I see it. That Negro—"

"Moses."

"From what I can tell, he lit out under cloak of darkness— stole a horse, to boot. He'll hang sure enough, believe you me."

Irving eyed the young lawman coolly over the rim of his glass.

"Then I suggest you catch him. The man must pay for what he's done."

"So when I seen what was goin' on in there, I rushed in with my butcher knife and let Mister Irving know he had to stop. But he was stronger than I would've thought for a man his size, and he threw me out. I run right back in, busting through that door, but he took my knife off me, and he stuck her with it—again and again. Most awful thing I've ever seen. He said I'd best clear out cuz he'd tell the law I done it." Mo's voice choked off, then returned in something close to a wheeze, "Poor Miss Lane, she had no idea what she was gettin' herself into!"

Cal sized up the man before him. "How long you been working for that Irving fellow?"

"Nigh ten years."

"You ever bring him anybody else he sent for?"

"Just pigs."

"How's that?"

"Them pigs! That's all he ever wanted. Never a human being!"

"Yeah," said Cal, wishing he knew what else to say. "I'm afraid I don't follow."

Mo shook his head and clenched his fists. "It's always been them pigs I brought to him, that's what I do, see? I'm his cook, I slaughter them hogs for 'im. But sometimes he wants 'em raw. I mean—" He lowered his voice. "*Alive.*"

Cal and Big Yap glanced at each other. Neither one liked where this was going.

"He'd have me bring him one, maybe a half-sized, sometimes a full-grown, and I'd let it loose in back of the theater, then shut the door. Believe you me, the noises that would come outta there? Was enough to make your skin crawl off!" He swallowed. "Same thing he done to that poor girl…"

Big Yap frowned. "You're saying this Irving fellow…tried to *eat* that young woman?"

"I caught 'im in the act! She weren't dead, not when I busted down the door and saw him chewin' on her. But she sure was gonna be dead soon. When he stabbed her, that's when I saw the light leave her eyes, like a flame gone out." He clenched his fists. "I didn't know what else to do, so I run off, fast as that mare could carry me—"

Cal cleared his throat. "There's only one thing to be done now. Go back to Green Valley and plead your case. The law needs to hear your side of the story."

"No! I can't go back, don'tcha see? They think I done it—they'll lynch me!"

"They won't with Yap and me riding by your side."

Big Yap nudged our hero. The two of them moved off a few yards, and Yap lowered his voice. "You believe him?"

Cal nodded, keeping an eye on Mo as the big man wept quietly with his chin to his chest.

"It's just his word against that Irving fellow's." Yap blew out a sigh. "The way the world is, unfortunately, white's always right. He won't stand a chance."

"That's why he needs us. We'll make sure justice prevails." Cal returned to Mo as Blossom arrived with the man's horse in tow, reins clamped between her teeth. "Mount up. We ride to Green Valley."

Mo blinked, impressed by the authority in the young man's tone. "Who are you, son?"

"He's Coyote Cal," Big Yap announced, stroking Blossom's neck with affection. "Someday, he'll be a famous hero. But today, he's gonna make sure you speak your piece to the sheriff."

Mo swallowed hard. He palmed each of his eyes to be rid of the tears and cleared his throat with a solemn nod.

Sheriff Morgan stood out front of his office as he addressed a mob of angry, gun-toting men mounted before him. Rumors were flying around town about a beautiful girl from Pennsylvania that had been murdered; and as if killing her wasn't bad enough, the fiend had gone and torn her up good before stabbing her to death.

"All right, men," Morgan said in a voice that rang loud and clear like a church bell. "We all know what happened last night. Mr. Irving saw it with his own eyes. Moses Gray killed Miss Lane in cold blood—"

"Don't forget what else he done to her!" one fellow called out. The men roared with vehement oaths.

Morgan held up a hand to quiet them. "Mr. Irving is offering a reward of one thousand dollars for the capture of Moses Gray, dead or alive, to be split among you. But I would take it as a kindness if you would do your best to bring him back here *alive* to face the charges against him and to stand trial—"

"What's it matter? We're gonna lynch 'im anyways!"

"That may very well be," Morgan countered. "But this is not the Wild West."

"Uh—I beg to differ, Sheriff!" Murmurs of dissent swept through the crowd.

"Green Valley is a *civilized* town, and I plan to see that man brought to justice—by the books." Morgan drew his revolver and swept the muzzle across his posse. "You do this right, or you don't do it at all. You got that?"

The men nodded sullenly. "Why ain't you ridin' with us, Sheriff?"

Morgan shifted his weight. "Can't. Piles acting up again." The men muttered their condolences as he holstered his shooting iron. "Now get on out of here!"

The posse spurred their horses into a gallop and thundered out of town.

It was Big Yap who first noticed the cloud of dust gathering on the horizon. It seemed to hover, then move with singular purpose across the plain in their direction. Coyote Cal knew at once what stirred it: horses, and plenty of them. He tapped his heels against Thunder's flanks, urging the mighty steed into a gallop in the opposite direction. A mile back, they'd passed a rocky ravine that cut through a verdant hillside. Big Yap and Mo followed close behind, and within minutes, they'd reached their destination.

"They've got us in their sights," Yap remarked as they dismounted behind a cluster of massive boulders.

"I'm counting on it." Cal surveyed the cliffs on either side of them. "We'll need to climb."

"No way our horses could ever make it," countered Mo.

"You underestimate them." Cal mounted up and urged Thunder onward through the ravine, dodging every rocky obstacle.

The distant sound of rifle fire met their ears, and a hail of bullets came whizzing through the air, ricocheting off the boulders around them. Cal guided his horse toward a narrow path that led up a steep hillside on the east end of the ravine. Sure-footed and brave, Thunder navigated the single track, placing one hoof in front of the other as Cal rode low in the saddle and encouraged him, patting the palomino's neck until he'd brought Cal to the top of the cliff.

The barren plateau afforded our hero no cover, so Cal quickly dismounted and flattened himself and Thunder against the sun-warmed earth. Big Yap and Mo remained pinned down at the entrance to the ravine below, hiding from the intermittent rifle fire with their heads ducked and their guns at the ready. If they dared to mount up and follow Cal, they'd risk hot lead in the back.

Cal kept a steady hand on Thunder's neck, calming the powerful horse and keeping him from jumping up at the sound of approaching gunshots. As the cloud of dust dissipated at the mouth of the ravine, revealing more than a dozen trigger-happy riders, Cal drew the Winchester from his saddle's rifle boot and pressed himself against the ground. He couldn't see anything down below; he couldn't see anything at all.

Until he lifted his face from the dirt.

"Men," said the leader of the pack in a voice that echoed like a politician's. "Somewhere in this rocky ravine before us cowers that Negro butcher we're after. Judging from the tracks, he's got company—accomplices, or mayhap bounty hunters aiming to claim our reward. Either way, it's gonna be dangerous. So if any of you wants to turn back, now's the time. Nobody's gonna call you yellow." He cleared his throat theatrically. "We'll just think it real loud."

The other men chuckled.

With great bravado, they spurred their mounts into a gallop down through the ravine—which wasn't smart at all. Half the men fell from their horses as the poor animals stumbled over unseen rocks and threw their riders into the air. The other half pulled up, jerking at the reins as they caught sight of Coyote Cal high above them with his Winchester at waist level, its muzzle angled toward any one of them.

"Now who might you be?" called up one of the riders, seemingly frozen in his saddle. His cohorts maintained similar statuesque postures, while the men who'd gone sprawling from their injured mounts lay bleeding with gashes to their heads and limbs.

"He's the dang hero of this story!" Big Yap cheered. Sawed-off shotgun at the ready, he advanced on the riders with confident, bowlegged strides. "You go for them shootin' irons of yours, we'll put lead in you sure as you're breathin'. Won't kill you, but you'll be hurtin' plenty."

"Who the hell are *you*?" said the rider.

"He's my sidekick," Cal called down, his voice echoing from the cliffs below him.

"Aren't you a little young to have a sidekick?" The man with the politician's voice rose to his feet from among the rocks and wiped his bloody face across one sleeve. "Tell me, son, where are you hiding the Negro?"

"I ain't hiding." Mo stepped out from behind a boulder with his six-gun pointed at the ground. "Cuz I ain't done nothin' wrong, Mr. Abrams."

Abrams bared his teeth in a tight smile. "Well now, Moses, how about we let the sheriff decide that." The other riders murmured among themselves. "You come along with us, and we'll make sure you get a fair trial."

"We'll be the ones escorting Mo back to your town," Cal said, pivoting on his heel to aim the Winchester at Abrams. "I'm giving you and your men a head start. I suggest you take it."

Abrams chuckled. "We have you outnumbered four to one, *boy.*"

"But we're on our feet," countered Yap. "While half your men are in need of some serious doctorin'. Besides, you see Cal up there with that rifle? And you all down here in this kill box? No sir, I wouldn't want to be standin' in your boots."

Abrams licked his teeth, glancing at his wounded men. His gaze hardened as he looked at Mo. "Sheriff wants you dead or alive, Gray. Don't make no difference to me." Murmurs of assent drifted through the posse.

"Change of plans," Cal said to Yap. "You both mount up and head for town. I'll make sure these gentlemen give *you* a head start."

"Now how exactly are you gonna do that?" sneered Abrams as Big Yap and Mo climbed into their saddles and backed out of the ravine, Yap with his shotgun still aimed at the leader of the pack. "You can't shoot all of us!"

Cal's Winchester fired, and Abrams went down with a wild shriek, cradling his leg where a spurt of blood had erupted like gushing spring water.

"Bind that up." Cal motioned with his rifle for one of the wide-eyed riders to tend to Abrams. To Yap, he said, "Go on. I'll catch up."

With a nod, Big Yap urged Blossom out of the ravine at a gallop with Mo close behind.

"After them!" Abrams hollered, but no one moved to follow his command. The riders looked at each other and up at Coyote Cal as if trying to figure out the situation. As most of them hadn't seen much in the way of an education past the second grade, they found matters to be fairly confusing at the moment.

But one of them spoke sense: "He's gonna shoot us."

"He can't get all of you, idiot!" Abrams roared. *YELLOW!* his mind echoed.

The other fellow snorted. "I sure as hell don't aim to be his next target."

As it turned out, Cal didn't have to shoot anybody else, and once he'd given Yap and Mo enough of a lead, he allowed the posse to leave. They exited the ravine with much less gusto than they'd arrived, but Abrams was as adamant as ever that they follow the Negro fugitive as fast as they could. And he left Cal with these parting words,

"You best never set foot in my town, boy. I'm gonna be mayor someday. And I'll see to it your neck gets stretched."

Without a word, Cal—now mounted astride Thunder—motioned with his Winchester for the riders to get moving. They did so, some of them riding double after ending their wounded horses with bullets to the brains. Cal watched the posse go, stirring up another cloud of dust in its wake.

Once they were half a mile away, he turned Thunder down the hillside and urged the mighty steed into a gallop. In a blur of speed, he managed to pass the posse, leaving the riders once again confused by the peculiar situation that greeted them; they'd never seen a horse move so fast, of course.

Eventually, Cal caught up with Big Yap and Mo. The posse had fallen more than five miles behind them by the time our heroes escorted Mo into Green Valley. Galloping down the main street toward the sheriff's office, they received many a curious stare from the townsfolk.

One of the more observant men cried out, "It's Mo!" and drew the pistol at his side.

Before he could pull the trigger, Cal brought out his six-gun and fired. The man yowled in pain, shaking his hand where the pistol had been shot clean out of his grip. An awestruck gasp swept through the townspeople who'd gathered.

Mo pulled up in front of the sheriff's office, but he didn't dismount with Cal and Yap. "Reckon I'll wait here," he said.

Cal looped Thunder's reins over the hitching rail and stepped onto the boardwalk. He holstered his Colt revolver, glancing back at the man with the smashed pistol—standing in the middle of the street and wringing his hand—to make sure nobody else in town got any bright ideas.

"We have to believe justice will prevail, Mo." Cal approached the office door and knocked.

A few seconds passed before the door swung inward and the sheriff blinked up into the late afternoon sun. The lawman seemed a bit startled by the appearance of the young stranger on his doorstep. Then he caught sight of Mo in the saddle of the stolen horse, and the sheriff's hand shot to his holster—but Cal was too quick. He gripped the lawman's arm and flattened it against his door.

"The law seems a bit high-handed in this town." Cal forcibly took the sheriff's gun from him and tossed it to Yap.

"Who the hell are you?" the lawman demanded, his face burning crimson to the tips of his ears. "If my deputies weren't already out looking for—"

"I've met your *deputies*, and if things go according to plan, we'll have matters settled before they return."

Standing in the sheriff's office on either side of the front door, Coyote Cal and Big Yap waited for Mr. William Irving to arrive. The sheriff had sent for the theater owner after hearing Mo's side of the story and begrudgingly agreeing that Irving was in need of some additional questioning.

Now Mo sat beside the sheriff's desk and fidgeted as they waited. Sheriff Morgan glared at Cal, still irate at the way the young stranger had thrown his weight around. It hadn't helped matters how Big Yap continued to refer to Cal as *the hero of this story*, whatever that meant. For now, the sheriff would go along with Cal's plans—at least until the posse showed up.

Minutes passed in silence until the door opened inward with a hesitant creak. Before Mr. Irving knew what was happening, Cal and Yap had dragged him inside and shoved him against the wall, pinning him there. With Cal's Colt jammed into his solid gut, he was in no position to resist.

"What's the meaning of this?" Irving demanded.

"That's a mighty old line, mister," Big Yap remarked, shutting the door. "And I should know—I've been around longer than a coon's age!"

Irving's eyes fell on Mo, seated beside the sheriff. Tossing caution to the wind, he wrestled free of our heroes' grasp and dove straight for the big man, brawny arms outstretched and fingers grasping for purchase on his throat. "Murderer!"

Cal slammed his fist hard across Irving's jaw, and the man crumpled onto his bad leg. Cal gripped Irving by the collar and hoisted him up off the floor. "Speak the truth, mister. Who killed that girl?"

The sheriff watched, unblinking, as the scene unfolded before him, unable to believe this stranger was prepared to accuse one of Green Valley's most upstanding citizens of murder.

Irving's bloodshot eyes shone in the lamplight. "Who the hell are you?"

"He's—!" Big Yap began.

The sheriff cleared his throat loudly. "They've taken Mo's side in this case, Mr. Irving, and they have a few questions for you. Honestly though, I don't know who they are." At a loss, he shook his head and sat down, hoping the posse would arrive at any moment.

"You couldn't let the fine folks of this town find out about your unseemly appetites." Cal narrowed his heroic gaze at the theater owner. "Have there been others, Mr. Irving? Or was she your first?"

Irving's eyes darted in a frenzy. "I don't know what you're talking about—"

"You didn't just kill that girl—which would've been bad enough. You had other things planned for her."

"She was going to star in my production—"

Cal shook the man. "Mo *saw* you!"

Moses Gray nodded. "You know I did, Mister Irving. I'd always bring you them pigs—"

"Shut up!" Irving shouted. "I give you a job for ten years, and this is how you repay me?"

"There's no law against eating raw meat in this town, is there, Sheriff?" Cal half-turned to regard Morgan.

"Uh-no, I suppose not." The sheriff swallowed. Perspiration stood out on his forehead.

"*Animal* meat, that is," Big Yap added.

"No…" Morgan frowned.

"But I'd wager folks eating other folks is looked down upon." Cal raised an eyebrow at the lawman.

"Are you suggesting that Mr. Irving—?"

"You saw her body. You tell me. If what Mo says is true, then this man's teeth should match the bite marks." Cal gave Irving a shake. "You're a real freak, aren't you."

Irving stared up at our hero and smiled, his lips pulling back to reveal teeth that seemed to grow in the lamplight, lengthening and narrowing at the tips into needle-sharp fangs—rows upon rows of them, like nothing our hero had ever seen in his life.

"You have no idea," Irving hissed.

Launching himself into the air, he broke free of Cal's grasp on him and dove headfirst at Mo, driving his chomping jaws toward the big man's throat. Stronger than anyone in the room, Mo gripped Irving by the shoulders and fought to hold him off, but the smaller man seemed to have tripled his strength, and it took both of our heroes and the sheriff's combined force to pull the deranged theater owner off his prey.

"You're all dead now!" Irving shrieked. Mo lent his strength to hold the man still, but it was all they could do to keep him on the floor. Fangs flashing and snapping, his jaws seeming to unhinge and expand, Irving screamed, "I can't control it! It won't let me go. The wendigo—it has my *soul!*"

"What's he goin' on about?" Yap grunted.

"Wendigo…" Mo's eyes widened. "He's possessed…by a *demon?*" He winced at the sight of the gnashing teeth. "It's the demon's hunger he's got to feed!"

Irving's head thrashed, whipping up and down, side to side. "The wendigo made me do it, I tell you. I'm not a monster!" A guttural roar erupted from the man's throat.

"Wish Pastor Mather was here," Cal managed, shoving Irving to the floor with all his strength. "I don't know anything about exorcisms."

"Shoot me, blow my head off!" Irving pleaded. "You've got to kill me before it's too late. I told you I can't control it!"

At that moment, the door to the sheriff's office burst open, and Abrams limped inside with a string of curses. Out of breath and caked in dust, he froze, staring at the scene before him.

"Get out!" said the sheriff, turning to gesticulate emphatically at his deputy.

With one less man to hold him down, Irving shot up from the floor and propelled himself through the air, diving face-first into Abrams midsection, tearing straight through him with a fountain of blood and viscera. Cal drew his Colt and fired, palming back the hammer with every round he pumped into the theater owner. Yap drew his shotgun from its scabbard, squeezing the trigger and chambering rounds as fast as he could. The sheriff fired his six-gun blindly as gun smoke filled the room so thick, nobody could see much of anything or even hear themselves think over the din of so many shots fired in the confined space.

When their weapons clicked empty and the smoke cleared, our heroes and the sheriff stood over what remained of Abrams, torn in two, and the body of Irving, a bloody mess that barely resembled the man he'd been. Mo stared in disbelief at what had become of his former boss.

"Guess we…won't need to hang him." Sheriff Morgan looked out the open door to where the posse stood gaping in the street like horrified statues. "You all are witnesses. It was…Irving who killed the girl last night—as well as Mr. Abrams…just now."

Cal holstered his Colt. "Can't say I expected things to turn out this way, but one thing I'm sure of. The arm of the law has no business reaching for this man." He gave Mo a pat on the back.

Mo nodded absently. "Thank you—for believing me."

"It pays to have a good ear for the truth." Tipping his hat to the sheriff, our hero stepped over the bloody mess with Big Yap close behind. They took their leave, climbing into the saddles of Thunder and Blossom and riding out of town while the dumbstruck posse gazed after them.

"Well, Cal, there you go again, vamoosing without collecting the reward we so justly deserved," Big Yap grumbled as they rode along. "I tell you, I could've done more than a sight with five hundred bucks! Iffin we would've split it evenly, that is. And it ain't as if we didn't earn it—gettin' shot at by that posse? Dealin' with a saw-toothed freak of nature? Now *that* should deserve some kind of reward, I've gotta say! But no, don't say nothin', I know already what it'll be. *Justice is its own reward*—or some such. And I agree with you most of the time, you know I do. But good ought to be rewarded as much as evil ought to be punished, don'tcha think?"

He had to pause for breath, as was usually the case during these tirades. He waited for Cal's reply, but the young man remained silent and pensive, gazing straight ahead.

Big Yap blew out a sigh. "Seein' Mo acquitted of all charges with a good chance of livin' the rest of his days on God's green earth—I reckon that's reward enough, when you come right down to it. Besides, it ain't like that Irving fellow could've paid us, seein' how he was guilty and all freakified there at the end…and *dead.*" He squinted at Cal with a sudden thought. "You think his demon died along with 'im?"

"I sure hope so, Yap."

Big Yap watched him for a moment. Seeing that Irving fellow transform into a demonic creature had been nothing short of horrifying. Cal was working through the bizarre experience in his own quiet way; he'd talk about it when he was good and ready. And Yap would be right there to listen when he did.

"Don't fancy the thought of it floating around looking for another host or some such." Big Yap shivered involuntarily. "Think we'll ever run across anything that peculiar again?"

Cal glanced at him with half a smile. "We'll have to wait and see. But I'm sure we're up to the challenge."

Yap snorted. So did Blossom. "Reckon we are, at that."

Urging their horses onward, our heroes rode into the blood-red glow of a glorious sunset, ready for whatever weirdness the morrow held in store for them.

PANNING IN THIN AIR

by Gerri Leen

She sat staring at me, her eyes the same cold gray as ever. "So, you found me."

It was a ludicrous comment. I always found her.

We had materialized in an old-fashioned building with marble floors and stained glass windows glowing in the red and gold tones she always loved. The glass threw colored shadows on the walls around us. She sat on the railing of one of the twin curving stairs, and a waterfall that should not have been in this place roared behind her, down the space between the stairways.

Water splashed at my feet; I moved so that my shoes didn't get soaked. "Let me guess. You've brought the Klondike River here?"

"It's washed up. Used up. Not like before." She peeked over the railing she was perched so precariously on. For a moment, it seemed as if she might topple over. I knew better than to try to help her. And it wasn't as if the fall would hurt her, any more than drowning would, or even my hands wringing the breath she no longer had from her throat.

"Oh, the river's still wet," I said, lifting up my right shoe so she could take in the mark her ghostly water had caused on my similarly ghostly shoes.

"Dried up, then. No gold left." She sighed, a movement that caused her ample chest to rise and fall in a way I'd always found titillating. That much hadn't changed; she was still the most exciting woman I'd ever known. "No gold," she said, pushing her fingers through the air, and a gold pan appeared. She poked through it, as if she was searching for the elusive, treacherous substance.

There was no shortage of gold on her. The gilded bangles I had given her so long ago adorned her wrists; a heavy gold collar she'd earned from milking the miners surrounded her lovely throat. She wore a ruffled peach gown that looked as if it had come straight from Paris. I didn't remember this gown—was she finally coming up with new things? Was her imagination breaking through her pain and need for revenge?

But it would not do to ask. Instead, I gave her a snide smile. "Let me guess. You need matching earrings?"

She shook her hair out of her face and I saw small gold studs in her earlobes.

"Larger ones, perhaps? It's not like you to go for something so simple."

"And you would know." She eased off the railing and walked toward me, water still splashing out of the gold pan she carried— only one? She normally carried several. "Why are you here?"

"To take you home."

"We have no home. You saw to that when you left me alone with my river and my gold."

I was discovering forgiveness was a harder thing to find than gold. I *had* left her, but it was over a century ago. Years that neither of us had lived through—unless you could call this haunting of each other that we did a life. "I love you. Please let this go."

Peals of harsh laughter echoed through the hallway, and I feared for the stained glass windows; her voice could shatter such fragile things. But she calmed before they could break.

That too was new.

"I'm tired," she said, her voice so hopeless I thought my heart might break.

"I'm tired, too. Can't we go home?"

"Where is home?"

Home should have been wherever she was, but I'd thrown that away. "I can show you."

"Is there gold there?"

"Yes." Or so some said. The streets lined with it and all that. But I was taking a chance—would we even be welcome in such a place?

Then again, taking chances had been what I'd excelled at. Except for taking a chance on her, on us.

"I could jump." She looked down past the waterfall; it would no doubt be a long way down. She always brought the dramatic with her.

"You could." She'd done it before. "Please, don't. I find it tiresome."

"Just as tiresome as you found me." She held out her arm, shaking it so the bangles tinkled. "This doesn't keep me warm, all this beautiful gold."

"No. It doesn't." I'd traded her for it, left her behind for the promise of more wealth than I could make staying up North. A rich life, spent with a coldly beautiful woman who had never loved me the way this one had.

"You didn't keep me warm, either."

"I can now. It's time to give up the gold. Put down the pan."

She stared at the pan. Seemed to finally realize that in the past she had come with so many more.

"Put it down, my dearest."

"Like this?" She put the pan on the ground but did not let go of it. "Do you love me?"

"Yes."

"Will you follow me? Never leave me?"

"Yes." I smiled and let my relief show.

It was a mistake.

"Prove it." She grabbed the pan and jumped lightly onto the railing. "Follow me some more." She stepped off.

I hurried over; her body was gone, as usual. But I could hear her laughter as she headed for some other place, where light streamed through red and gold glass and made her think of our old home.

But she was changing. She was…softening. This couldn't last forever, could it?

I sighed and followed her.

JUNCTION, TEXAS

by Joshua Gage

The Stranger pulled into town in that thin strip of twilight between literal sundown and absolute night, the hour when shadows crawl forth like tears of makeup down a whore's face. He came down from the desert, but was as pale as a newly woven sheet, almost as though he had never been touched by the sun despite coming from miles of barren earth, and his skin had a thick, oily sheen to it, like he'd painted himself over in bacon grease. He strolled to the local hotel, and slapped down enough money for a week's worth of food and lodging, never saying a word. Ezekiel Masterson, the innkeeper, handed him a heavy iron key on a ring, and beckoned the stranger to follow him up the stairs to the room.

In cities along the coast—Galveston, Lavaca and suchlike—there is a saying, "The sea spits up what it can't keep down." It is a game among the local children to scrounge along the beaches after a mighty storm to see what treasures can be found. Sometimes it's nothing more than drift wood, occasionally painted pieces of a smashed boat worn smooth by the sea. Occasionally, something larger will be found—a coin, perhaps, crusted over with salt, and Jimmy Donnegan and his brothers, Micah and Kevin, once found a whole iron gate, still chained and locked, rust covered but still heavy and solid enough that it took all three of them to lug it back to their house. They begged their mother to keep it, but she refused, telling them what they all knew already—"The sea spits up what it can't keep down"—and demanding that they return it to the beach. Then there are the bodies, usually a dog or a cat, sometimes a bird, bloated and deformed by the water and the waves, usually half stripped of hair. The children take turns poking these curiosities with a stick, half wishing that the swollen corpse will do something, burst like a ripe melon or let out one last defiant noise of life before truly dying, and half insuring themselves and their dreams that it won't.

The Stranger surveyed the sparse room, nodded, and took the key from Masterson's shaking hand. He then turned and without speaking a word to Masterson or even locking the door behind him, drifted down the stairs and out into the street.

The Right Honorable Gideon D. Newcoms held no actual degree in divinity or similar educational background. Gideon had been blessed with a most powerful voice and an aptitude for linguistic gymnastics that had served him well despite his lack of formal education. Armed with only a copy of Noah Webster's *A Compendious Dictionary of the English Language*, Gideon had set out to take the world into his hands by way of other people's hard-earned money. In a previous life, he had been the learned physician Dr. Dudley J. Hadacol, curer of contagions, physician to frailties, healer of ill health, and purveyor of potions with proven power over any plague or pathos known to man. One day, in the mining town of Bright Prospect, he had been cornered and called out by the townsfolk as both a liar and a thief, and was on his way to a pot of boiling pine tar and a sackful of chicken feathers when the mob was silenced by a preacher who held up a Bible and, with a loquaciousness that spellbound even Gideon, turned them away. Once the people had dispersed, the preacher turned on Gideon, who had been crawling in the dirt to escape the angry rabble. Silhouetted by the sun, the man stood over Gideon, but did not admonish him. He simply held out his Bible and said "Go in peace to love and serve the Lord." Ever since that moment of joyous revelation, Gideon used his oracular talents not for personal gain, but to spread the word of God.

"Seek ye not Satan in the dens of iniquity!" Gideon bellowed from his chosen corner that afternoon. "Seek not the nocturnal delights of the prairie nymphs that lie in wait, seek not the incubus of gold found on their gambling tables. Did not our Lord raze Sodom and Gomorrah to the ground for their lasciviousness; did He not punish the Israelites for their idolatry for the golden calf? Surely I tell you, just as he drowned the armies of Egypt in the Red Sea, so too shall he drown you at the tables of faro. My brothers and sisters, I have seen the signs! A red moon riseth in the east! I tell you, Judgment Day is at hand. The Lord shall come down from heaven and only the righteous shall be saved. Are you ready, my brothers and sisters? You, sir," and here Gideon punctuated his prophecies with a thin, gnarled finger aimed at the Stranger, "are you prepared for the coming of our Lord? When the seas begin to boil and the dead begin to walk, will your soul be saved?"

"It's a little late for that, Preacher," said the Stranger, and he aimed himself straight for the saloon, where he placed a single coin on the bar, enough for a tumbler full of whiskey, which Troy Simmons poured generously. The Stranger was slow to retrieve his glass, and when he did, he simply held it, rarely bringing it to his lips as he leaned upon the bar, surveying the establishment and watching the performance on the stage.

Buffalo Sal was not from Buffalo, her name was not Sal, and despite the implications of the songs she sang, never had she danced by the light of the moon. She had been christened Emily Louisa Phillips, and hailed from a small farmstead outside of Lubbock. She had run away from home when she was thirteen, hoping to make it all the way to St. Louis or San Francisco, where she could start a new life, away from pigs and cows and red dirt that would never be able grow anything even if it had wanted to. She learned quickly that the men who drove wagons or coaches had limited uses for a woman, and that her cleaning, sewing or cooking skills paled in comparison to other more lucrative activities. By the time she was fifteen, she looked as though she were twenty-three, and had made it as far as Junction, where she settled in with a professional contract under Troy Simmons, The Leather Gentleman.

It was rumored that Troy's name came not from the Simmons Leather Business, which his father started north in Cleburne, but from his habit of punishing the women under contract who displeased him by strapping them to his bed and flogging them bloody; however, this was merely speculation the part of the townsfolk, who occasionally heard shouts and muffled noises erupting from his bedroom window, which looked out over the main thoroughfare. It was Simmons's habit to dress in a full ditto suit at all times, even donning the long coat and matching vest in the height of summer when the sun could sweat the scales off a rattlesnake, and he was rarely seen without his top hat. He fancied himself a true English Gentleman, though he had never been to England, and sought to emulate this role in every aspect of his life. Despite his near obsessive Anglophilia, he could never get the accent right, and often succumbed to his northern Texas drawl.

When he wasn't negotiating a business deal meant to secure his position in town as unofficial and unelected mayor, head of commerce, real estate mogul or half a dozen other titles which didn't exist but would be defined as Troy Simmons if they had, Simmons would be found managing his saloon and brothel, The Iron Pig. Positioned between the general store and the telegraph office, which also housed the town's irregular newspaper, and directly across the street from the sheriff's office and jailhouse, Simmons had positioned himself at the center of all of the town's information, business, and criminal activities, all of which he directly or indirectly supervised and managed. Were an omnipotent observer to peel back the layers of illicit activity, from crooked card games to cattle rustling, drug smuggling to murders, that plagued Junction and kept it as wild as a town could be without tearing itself to dust, sooner or later they would find that the core was always Troy Simmons.

The Iron Pig rarely emptied, even when it was officially closed, and weekends were especially inundated. With all the bodies crammed into such a small space, most of them saturated with alcohol and sweating from the day's heat and hard labor, it seemed to Sal that every man from here to Llano had decided to stop and drink in Junction that night. Still, she aimed to make that evening's performance as sultry and igniting as possible, crooning and dancing her way through versions of George Frederick Root favorites, ending with a throaty version of the classic "The Yellow Rose of Texas" that would make even the most staunch and ardent of ministers do interesting things between their navel and their knees.

Simmons tended to shut The Iron Pig down only when the beer and whiskey stopped selling and the majority of his painted doves had their johnnies cooed for the night. While there were always a few stragglers, Simmons tended to get everyone gone by three or four o'clock in the morning, rolling those few drunks who had collapsed into the shadows and the corners out into the street then searching their pockets for anything valuable. He never had a problem getting anyone who could stand on his own two feet out of the building, and if he did, there was a heavy cane of Irish oak stashed under the bar, a razor blade tucked in his boot, and a Cogswell Pepperbox in his holster to answer for any unlikely possibilities. The Stranger had camped at the end of the bar all night, the same mug of horse piss resting in front of him, barely touched.

"I do hate to be rude," Simmons said in his best affected accent, "but as owner and proprietor of this establishment, I fear that I must either ask you to procure one of our other purveyances for yourself this evening, or else remove yourself from this location." The Stranger cocked an eye a him, then took a long, slow draft of his whiskey, nearly emptying the glass. Simmons was nonplussed, but rallied himself almost immediately, dropping his accent on the way. "Look, partner, either buy yourself a slice of minge or you're up and out. We're closing for the night."

The Stranger pulled a Cavalry Issue M1873 from his holster, and pointed it directly at Buffalo Sal, who was lingering in the doorway. More often than not, on nights when no one else rented her affection, she found herself in the bed of Troy Simmons, who took his cut right off the top, but treated her nice enough and still paid her enough to live on, if not save for a rainy day. "I see sir has discerning taste," said Simmons, returning to his British accent, "Nothing but the best for sir."

The Stranger shook his head. "Contract," he said.

"Ah, sir," said Simmons quickly, "the bodies here are meant merely as a temporary comfort, with reasonable contract prices, not as a permanent purchase."

"Contract," the stranger said again, this time pointing the gun at Simmons, cocking the hammer in the process.

"Look, partner," Simmons said, taking a step towards the barrel and slamming his fist down on the bar, "I've been patient enough. Now you're playing a game you can't win. I've had plenty a gun pointed at me afore, and I'm here to tell you I'm still standing, and those doing the pointing ain't. It's time for you to bottle up and go, and if I was you, I wouldn't seek potation or solace in this establishment again, if you get my drift. I don't take kindly to threats."

It is a well known fact that Texas has its own laws, written and unwritten. The penalty for breaking these laws is steep, and can often be found at the end of a rope, if one is lucky. The town of Junction used to have a lawman by the name of Lawrence Jensen, official with a star, but he ran afoul of Troy Simmons, which is a death warrant of its own sort. Still, the folks who saw the showdown say it took four bullets, all in the chest, to drop Jensen. Simmons claimed the body, and that was the last anyone saw of it, officially. Rumor has it that, once Simmons was done having his fun, the body was so badly burned and beaten that it was impossible to tell who it belonged to. There are those who say that Simmons buried it in one uncharacteristic act of Christian charity, but others insist that he simply dragged it to the river, loaded it down with a rock, and let the fish and water do whatever they wanted to with it.

Buffalo Sal had only cried twice since she visited Junction, as any girl working the business long enough learns to calcify her skin and cage what few vulnerabilities she has. The first time she was working independent, and a drunk johnnie beat her so badly that she lost a back tooth and couldn't work for two weeks. Troy Simmons visited with her one evening, while she was nursing a swollen cheek with a cold rag and self-pity. He offered her his contract, promising not to work her too hard until she turned eighteen and to protect her from any man who tried to do this sort of thing again to her.

The second time was when she watched Troy Simmons shoot down Lawrence Jensen, who had always been sweet on her. Since she first laid eyes on Jensen, she had always dreamt that, one day, she would be able to buy her way out of her contract and that the two of them would be wed. Troy Simmons had stolen that dream, and despite his unusually kind treatment to her, Buffalo Sal always kept a small coal of pure hate smoldering in her heart.

The Stranger proceeded to pull a giant Bowie knife from the sheath at his belt and stab it into the stained wood of the bar. Spreading the fingers of his right hand wide on the bar top, he began to dance the knife point between them, his eyes never leaving those of Troy Simmons. "A challenge," he said, "First blood."

When it came to hard, pointed objects, be they knives, bullets or his own priapic organ, Troy Simmons had an affinity for them and a natural aptitude. It was insulting to watch this stranger belittle and challenge him in his own establishment, even if the bastard was scraping for any toe hold to fight back with. With a sneer, Troy Simmons slammed his hand back on the bar and whipped out his own knife. "This, sir," he said, returning to his attempt at an English accent, "is a genuine Sheffield hunting knife, imported all the way from England, and thus is in every way superior to your American Bowie. First blood it is, sir, and may God have mercy on the loser's soul." He began dancing the blade between his fingers, matching the stranger's relaxed and easy tempo.

The rules of the challenge were simple enough, and it was a game known to any school boy in the country. The opponents were to keep a certain pace, stabbing their knife blade into the open spaces between their spread fingers without actually cutting themselves in the process. If either player accelerated their pace, their opponent would have to match suit or forfeit. The first player to either cut himself or not keep up with their opponent would automatically lose.

Simmons quickly accelerated the pace, the black length of his Sheffield barely seeming to move as its point tapped between his spread fingers. To his credit, the stranger kept pace, their two blades echoing a dull percussive rhythm throughout the now empty bar.

Buffalo Sal watched from the hallway as the two men dueled over the rights to her body. She held her breath, partially insulted that her life had fallen so low as to be the prize in a boy's game between two men, partially terrified at what would happen to her if either one of them won. Some women might be flattered to have grown men dueling it out over them, but Sal had known enough men in her life to understand that the things men fought fiercest for were almost always the things that mattered least in the long run.

The Stranger looked over at Sal, smiled assuredly, and winked. Then he winced as his knife nicked his pinky finger, scrapping most of the skin from his second knuckle with it.

Troy whooped and flipped his knife, catching it blade first before sliding it back into his boot. "Son," he said, his authentic drawl rising in a rush of adrenaline, "I've got to hand it to you. When you fall down, you fall down fighting. Still, a fall you have taken and I'm not the one to clean you up. Now, get the hell out of my joint before I get you out."

The Stranger stared at Sal for a moment, then turned back to Troy. He reached in his coat pocket and pulled out a small sack which he tossed on the bar. "Double. I win, I get the contract. You win, well, I guess I'll walk out of here by myself."

"Son," said Troy, shaking his head, "you must be thicker than the air at noon in the middle of July. C'mon now, you've lost. Let it go, man."

The Stranger reached for his bag. He had barely lifted it from the bar when he whispered, "Chickenshit," under his breath, loud enough for Troy to hear.

Troy's hand rattlesnaked out, slamming the stranger's hand and the bag on the bar. "What did you say?"

"You heard me," the stranger said coolly. "You lucked out once, but I bet you don't again. In fact, I'll raise the stakes. I'll use my other hand."

"You come in to my place of business," snarled Troy, "challenge me, lose, then insult me? You must be too stupid to pour piss out of a boot with a hole in the toe and directions on the heel. I have every right to shoot you where you stand, and no one would be the wiser."

"I would," said Sal, striking a match against her dress button and lighting a cigarette, "and you would. And no matter who else knew, it would be enough that the two of us witnessed the day when the mighty Troy Simmons backed down from a fight and shot a man instead. C'mon, Troy," she said with a viperous smile that would convince a train to jump its tracks and try the dirt road, "you beat him once. What do you have to lose?"

Troy removed his hand from the stranger's, whipped his knife from his boot, flipped it high into the air so that it plummeted down and stuck to the bar with a sharp, deep sound, and slammed his hand down, fingers sprawled around its still quivering steel. "Draw your blade."

Sal watched as the game began, gently at first, with a slow rhythm that reminded her of rocking back and forth in a hammock. Still, men will be boys, and soon the pace accelerated to a dull, monotonous pounding that Sal knew only too well. She shook her head knowingly—men apparently learned nothing from music and dancing, and had no sense of pacing, no variation in speed and tempo. It was slow until they got excited, then furious and fast until they were done, and then a long, snoring stop when they exhausted themselves.

There are occasions in life when time seems to draw itself as long and thin as possible and everything dwindles to an absolute stillness, like dust clinging to a beam of sunlight. Looking back on that moment, Buffalo Sal swore that as she watched the knives, she knew that they were going faster and faster, but saw that they were slowing down, until she could measure each stab into the bar with her hand on her thigh, almost like keeping beat to a song. She would always tell anyone who would listen that watching the stranger's blade was like watching an autumn leaf flow down a calm stream until it gets caught against a rock, painting its dark and wet surface a bright crimson, the same way that the stranger's blade did when, instead of landing between his fingers, it landed in the back of Troy Simmons's hand, pinning it to the bar itself.

Sal didn't scream. She could have, and probably should have, but she didn't. It was Troy who screamed, his hand stuck to the bar top, his body reeling around like a crazed dog leashed to a tree, with only that frail bond between body and wood keeping the beast from killing everything in sight. The stranger stood up, stepped back from the bar, and drew the Cavalry Issue M1873 from its holster. His hand worked slowly, easing back the hammer and squeezing the trigger, until all six cartridges had been emptied into Troy Simmons.

When she was sure that he was dead, Sal stepped behind the bar, straddled Troy's corpse, yanked up her skirt hem with one hand. "I assume," she said, as a yellow stream of urine broke forth from between her legs and splashed across Troy's body, "that you think you own me now. Well, I've worked for one man, and I ain't about to work for another." With that, she pulled a double-barreled Derringer from between her breasts. "I know you think you're some kind of slick with that blade of yours, but I figure that at this range," she jabbed the gun into the Stranger's chest, "I have more than enough time to squeeze before you can cut me."

"I don't want your contract," the Stranger said, pushing away the Derringer slowly. "It's all over. There's nothing to worry about anymore. You're done now. You can go home."

Sal laughed, a big guffawing laugh that leapt from her belly and out of her mouth before she knew it was even in her. "Home?" she sneered, "What do you know about my home?"

"I know there are people in Lubbock who miss you. I know that they love you. I know they don't care what you've done as long as you come back to them, safe and healthy. Take that," he said, nodding at the sack of coins still on the bar, "and buy whatever you need. It's yours. I know this isn't what you ever wanted, and now it's over."

"Yeah, it seems like you know a whole bunch for someone I've never even met. Hell, I don't even know your name."

The stranger, pulled open his shirt. There, punctuating the thin lines scattered liberally across his chest, like buzzards resting on telegraph wires, were four round, white bullet scars. "Yes," he whispered, "you do."

CHIKCHEEREE

by Paul Lorello

You grow up in Adam County and sooner or later you hear some chaw-sucking old-timer spinning about "them hellbound critchers up on the ridge." That kind of talk bores into the skulls of some your softer types, like Kenny. As for me, superstition was the least of my worries. The horses got splints half way up. I would have shot both of them and had us go the rest of the way on foot had I not been afraid of the noise disclosing our location. Not to mention we had to save our bullets. Not to mention there was always the chance we could use one of beasts for meat if we needed.

And then there was the salient fact that we were tired. There's a kind of tired that gets into the center of your bones and fists up till your muscles just stop moving, and your mind starts telling you things you can't bear to hear: like you need to drop and sleep—now—even though a posse of ten or twelve men not more than a mile behind you would like nothing better than to string you up and watch you kick, because you left the deputy sheriff gasping in a pool of it. One day, I thought, one sweet day Kenny and I would get a chance to argue about which one of us actually shot the man. All I know's there was suddenly shouting, and Kenny took a dame by the hair, and a child screamed—I can't shoot children—but there was a crowd of men and I blasted into that crowd. And then a holy blaze of gunfire and screaming that sounded like all twelve angels had come down to show us a new destruction of Jericho. Kenny let go of the dame and we blasted, and good men fell, and there were sprays of blood and someone shouted that the deputy was down. And that's when we took off with about a pound of gold each.

We dropped in a cave in the rocks on the ridge. There was a pool of still water about ten feet across. Don't know if you ever smelled a cave with such a pool. It's a cold smell, and harder than pine, but it practically begs you to close your eyes and breathe deep until you go unconscious. It was quiet as tombs up there too, which was advantageous. We'd gotten a good mile jump on the posse, and in the dead quiet we'd hear their approach for sure.

"We gotta move, Hathorne," Kenny said suddenly.

I leaned up on my knees. "And just where you reckon we gotta move to?"

"Anywhere but here. Sun's going down."

"You don't say."

"I reckon you ain't afeared o' no critchers?"

"Mountain lions?"

"Spider folk," he said weakly.

I don't think he saw my grin. I closed my eyes and leaned back. "Never hearda them."

"Didn't no one ever tell you about the nekkid lady who floats?"

"Do tell."

He licked his lips, and he kinda shivered and looked around. "Well, it goes that there was this Shawnee girl, went by the name of…" He stopped and licked his lips again. "Chikcheeree."

"That don't sound like no Shawnee name."

"Shet up and let me tell it. It's an old name. They don't use it no more. Chikcheeree, she fell in love with a brave, see? But he was already betrothed to another. So she prayed to the gods and they turned the other girl into a spider and sent her up here into the rocks to live out her years. Now because them gods did as Chikcheeree asked, they demanded a sacrifice from her. But Chikcheeree refused, because she figgered the gods musta sent that other squaw to torment her in the first place. Well, the gods ain't too crazy when us humans demonstrate our prideful nature and lack of humility in any fashion. So you know what they did?"

"I'm itchin' like a weasel in the hay to hear the rest of this."

"Well then, they went and turned the lover into a spider too, see, and sent him into the rocks to live with the other girl. When Chikcheeree found this out, she wept and wept, and they say that's how the creek in the valley was formed, and that's why they call it Weeping Creek, you hear?"

"Fascinating," I said.

"Well, damn it, it is fascinating. Well, day came when Chikcheeree had enough weeping, and that's when she went up into the rocks to kill the lovers. She searched high and low, searched every damned cave up in this here ridge and couldn't find them. She searched until she dropped and drowned in one of the cave pools. But because of her prideful and jealous nature, the gods doomed her spirit to haunt these pools. They say on the full moon she rises out of the water and floats there, nekkid as ol' Eve. And that's when the spider folk, the descendants of those two cursed lovers, they come out of the rocks and git you, cuz you're too busy looking at the nekkid girl in the water you don't see 'em comin'. The spider folk drink your blood and steal your bones away to build their temple. And they leave your skin on the cave floor to rot."

"And this is what you're afeared of?"

"Listen, stories develop for a reason. Even old wives' tales got reasons behind them."

I stood up and stretched. "This all makes for good campfire talk, but it don't seem plausible. No girl can cry that many tears. And besides, tears are salty and that there crick is freshwater. And it just don't make any sense anyway. Turning folks into spiders."

"Spider folk. Not regular spiders."

"And I'm telling you it ain't plausible. Like Navajos dancing to make rain. Ain't no god or gods up there watching over us, let alone watching us dance. It just ain't plausible."

"You go on talking like that," he said, turning his head toward the pool like he was avoiding my breath. "Just go on, and you'll see what happens to you."

"Listen," I said, and I wasn't feeling even a ghost of my patience anymore. "I once seen a family of cougars tear apart a pack of coyote pups, all except the runt. And you know why? Because the runt was all white, and his brothers and sisters weren't, and so he was able to hide in the snow. And I got to thinking that it could just as well start a family and have pups like itself, all good at hiding and surviving in the snow. Now if that pup can do it, then it don't matter if any other creature is born with two heads or five legs or what have you. If two heads suits it, it'll survive to breed. I reckon there's some pretty strange things out there, but ain't nothing magical about any of them. So you keep a-wardin' off spider folk and other goblins. You know what I'm worried about? I'm worried that there's someone in that posse that thinks the same way I do and ain't afeared to come on up in the dead of night, track us to this very cave, and blow us to hell in our sleep. I'm afeared they'll have kids that'll grow up and think like they do, 'cause I intend on outliving them no matter what. Get it?"

"I git it."

"Now, way I see it, if there's a chance of even one of them coming up here after nightfall, it's good sense for us to sleep in shifts. We ain't outta this yet."

"Ok," he said, "but I still reckon your ideas are a tad wanting."

I walked up and hovered over him. "Listen to me, you crawlin' mouse, I ain't a-takin' any sleep if I know you're keeping lookout for some nekkid Shawnee girl instead of real threats to our safety. I swear on my life I'll blacken your whole face afore the night's done if you give me reason. Goddamn you, boy, look at you. Not twenty-three years on this earth and already y'like an old, fartin' granpappy tellin' tall tales for to keep his boney jaw from a-flappin' all by itself. Now buck up afore I whup your chin with the grip of my knife."

Without another word between us, I settled down. It was still early June, not yet time enough for the day haze to gather up and choke off the chill of night. Moonlight the color of lightning splashed all around us, and splashed across the water, and its reflection was a fat, dull jewel right in the center of the pool.

I wrapped myself in a skin and sat down with my back against the wall, and everything in me just let go to the fast-falling night and the sweet smell of the rocks. The last thing I saw afore my lids closed was Kenny all wrapped up in a mangy skin, chuffing hot breath into his hands.

When I opened my eyes, the moon was brighter than ever, and there was something that wasn't quite right about the air. I don't know what, but something unwholesome had crept through our little camp while I slept, and it left behind a wake fulla dread. How can I describe it other than that it was thick and warm, and that it wormed through the chill night air, and that it was vaguely like gun oil. Then I saw Kenny a-sleepin' like a little baby doll on the other side of the pool. I damned him once, and all the blood in me boiled up to my eyes, and I was just about ready to leap across'n' thrash him awake with my belt, when the dull jewel in the center of the pool dissolved like a mist, and something rose to the surface.

Nekkid and a-spreadeagle she was, her arms resting behind her head. I musta made a sound, I don't know, but I know I wanted Kenny to wake up, cuz I tore my eyes away from the girl and looked over at him.

But what was once Kenny was now nothing but an empty burlap sack of a man, one that resembled my friend some far-off way. He looked like a dried-up dog that lay in the sun for weeks on end. The vision brought a kinda crazy laugh into my head, a cacklin' old witch of a laugh that had gotten trapped beneath my scalp and wanted out. I turned my gaze back at the girl in the water, and a gust of a breath came out of my lungs that almost burst my throat. She had no face. And all her body underneath it, all that nekkid reddish brown flesh, it was all a blank stamp, with a dark patch between the legs that was just that and nothing more, and nothing revealed there except for more shadow, like who or whatever made her didn't know what a real human woman was supposed to look like and was working offa some picture in a medical man's notebook. Her flesh rippled and puffed, like'n she used her whole body to breathe.

That's when the smell in that cave suddenly became something that called to me. It was old, and warm, and it made me want to be there inside it. It filled my head with the lightest, sweetest air I'd ever known. And it was the deepest hunger and the rawest lust whatever roared inside a man when she floated over to me, and floated up over the water, her legs above me. Then she came down a bit, hovering there, and that patchy shadow between her legs settled before my eyes.

That's when she blotted out a patch of moonlight. And that's when I saw what was *around* her.

No mistakin' the haloed form of a giant spider.

But what should have been a discernible critter's body was nothing but a mass of jellied glass. The only thing that had any visible substance were the guts. I shudder when I think of the forces that forged this thing over the ages, how over tens of thousands, maybe millions of years, a slow and silent hand sculpted those innards to resemble a nekkid woman. But the thing that haunts me to this day was the fact that she smelled so nice. That frightened me even more than the sound she made in the hollows of that ridge: a clicking of the fangs, and then a spurt of venom that went sizzling toward the ground: *chk-cheee-reeee...*

I screamed then, I think, I must have, because the thing reared its hindquarters and the faceless girl sat up.

All I know's I had one option, the one that got me here in the first place: I drew my piece and emptied it into the face of that monster. It spurted blood and venom in a hateful hiss.

I didn't kill it, but I wounded it pretty bad. I seized the opportunity to escape.

I saw torches speckling the landscape like some herd of vengeful ghosts marauding through the night. There was folks in that posse did think like me after all.

"I know I take my chances coming up here."

I swung around and pointed my piece toward the voice. The holy man stopped where he was and reached for his Heaven. His black vestments were dappled with dried mud and bits of bramble weed, like'n he'd taken a tumble or two on the way up. He had that soft, pink look that all Reverends have. Even where his scalp was exposed was unweathered.

"Any man who fires on women and children probably has no compunction in regards to firing on a Reverend," he said.

I didn't answer this accusation.

He lowered a hand to wipe his brow, then raised it again. "Word was sent by wire to Arkansas. They's a-waitin' for you there."

I hadn't even thought of that possibility. Gold blinds a man to his own fortune. And somehow this new hopelessness didn't weigh very much.

"You know what's in that there cave, Reverend?"

"I've heard things," he said, his voice like an old fiddle.

"Well then, I got a choice: Either stay up here and git eaten alive or go down there and hang."

"There's always salvation."

"For you, Reverend. Not for me."

"Are you going to kill me, son?"

I laughed, because it suddenly struck me how, holy man or heathen, in the end all our priorities are the same. It took a minute for me to wipe the tears from my eyes, and to stop my whole body from shaking, and to chase every bad thought I ever had outta my soul.

"The Lord's got a terrible vengeance, son, but also the most loving embrace for those who accept him."

The holy man waited patiently while I pressed my fingers into my eyes and took a breath to steel myself up. "Reverend, the reason why I don't want to go back to that beloved of Hell in there is because if'n I go, I just might want to stay. You see, there's a call of lust about it. You being a man of what they call moral

fortitude, I figure if there's anyone who'll be able to stand it...
well, Reverend, I need you to shoot that thing when I drag it out."
I held out my piece, barrel first.

"I cain't shoot one of God's creatures."

I laughed in his old, pious face. "One o' God's critchers,
Reverend, and I'm a-gonna rope it. Besides, it ain't just the
critcher. I want you to shoot me too if'n that thing gets the best
of me. Understand?"

He shook his head 'no,' but I knew if'n it came down to it
and that thing had me in its jaws, that preacher'd have no trouble
sending us both to our dark sleep in a lizard's wink. And wouldn't
you know it, he took the piece.

I went back into the ridge and damn near staggered when
I saw it. Its rear half—and that woman's head—was drooping
down into the water. I steeled my heart and jumped in behind it.

The freezing water bit through me. I screamed and cursed at
the thing as I wrapped a rope around its tree branch legs. There
were fine hairs all up and down it that felt like corn silk. Its leg
pulsed with life and thrashed out of my grip a couple of times,
as the critcher sprayed hisses of milky venom every which way. I
got a hold of one rear leg and wrapped a loop around it. Then I
pulled in the opposite direction so that the leg swung underneath.
I wrapped the rope around one of the legs on the other side and
I jumped on top of its back, rope in hand.

I almost passed dead away, smelling that beautiful stink and
staring at that gorgeous female form writhing in its bubble of
crystal flesh.

Getting a grip on the cave floor, I pulled, and the spider flipped.
Underneath was as clear as the rest of it, with the womanly body
looking like a dress dummy underneath. The guts twitched as I
pulled up and got my bearings. Then I hoisted the rope over my
shoulder.

The horses reared and shrieked like they seen the devil hisself
being drug behind me. The preacher crossed himself with his
free hand.

There in the moonlight, there were shadows flickering around, like when a candlewick gets too long. I looked back and saw the spider, its clear-coated legs dancing in the air, a spray of bloody venom in misty, pink clouds around its head, and that brown nekkid woman twisting in the night.

"For the love of Christ, Reverend!" I screamed.

I ain't never seen a man's hand shake like that preacher's grip on my Colt. Like a fish tail in whitewater.

But he shot that nekkid girl through the heart. Then I took the gun and finished her.

After a breath, I'll be damned if that preacher didn't try to convert me still through his tears.

"See here, you blubberin' old coot," I said. "I'm a-headin' on over this here ridge to fields of wild wheat and honeysuckle. I can go in any direction I want and no one'll see me. 'Less that posse down there can fly, I say I'm home free. I trust we can keep the sanctity of the confessional up in these rocks, padre?"

He looked around and down over the scramble of boulders below. Then he looked at me. "What posse you talking about?"

I had only noticed then that there were no more lights. Nothing but moon shadows. "Well now, they sure tuckered out early, didn't they."

The preacher straightened, and his voice became sermon strong. "That wasn't a posse, son, that was a funeral camp. We buried three men, including the deputy, and one woman. I left those grieving folk to come up here and persuade you to justice. Once you made your way into this here ridge, they figured that was it. They wired Arkansas just in case."

"In case, what?"

"In the unlikely event you made it outta here alive. You're young, son, and have no idea what the older folk've seen."

I let what he said sink in a moment. Even if he was wrong about there being other critchers up here, I knew with the surety of smoke on fire that this here spider, like all critchers on earth, had to mate. Which meant that there had to be others like it. And if'n they're like all living things, and the cruel forces that drive them work the way they tend to do, well, sooner or later they'll go lookin' outside of caves for mates. And on accounna they probably mount each other like dogs, and they got that design to them, well, it's just a matter of time afore they...

In the name of my mama, I couldn't finish that thought.

I decided I'd talk to some of the more learned among those who'd sooner see me dead, maybe convince them to let me help them hunt down every last one of these monsters until we're all safe.

On the way down, I was silent, and so was the Reverend. I wanted to tell him about the cougars and the white pup. But I didn't. If'n no one bought my sincerity, I'd have to have something to chat about afore my walk to the gallows.

THE TWO OF GUNS

by John F.D. Taff

Dust.

Dust and heat dominated the desert stretched before Gus without an end in sight. The frisky bay he'd stolen had slowed some miles before, as the land ahead began to look exactly like the land behind.

Gus reined in the horse amid a cloud of dust. He produced a frayed bandanna from his shirt pocket, mopped sweat and dust from his balding head. He rubbed his eyes and scanned the horizon.

To the northeast, through a shimmering curtain of heat, he saw a small tail of brown dust wagging in the afternoon sky.

Sheriff Holloran and his posse.

Not getting closer, but certainly not falling behind.

He'd left Wilson Ridge in a hurry after shooting a man in the bar following an exchange of pleasantries concerning each others' questionable family lineage and dubious personal habits. He didn't remember what brought it on, didn't even know if he'd killed the man, though the posse chasing him was a good indication that funeral arrangements were pending. He had left so quickly that he dropped his gun on the way out of town and didn't turn back to get it. Doing the two-step at the end of a rope didn't appeal too much to Gus, no sir.

The horse neighed in impatience. He yanked the reins,

slapped the horse on the rump. The bay took off with a slight, disapproving whinny and a skitter of hardscrabble.

He leaned over in the saddle to spit, but thought better of it. He might be out here long enough to curse every mouthful of liquid he had spat without care into the dust. He swallowed carefully, gave the horse a sharp spur.

He rode for another hour before he caught sight of something moving up ahead. After a couple of minutes, Gus was able to tell that it was a wagon; not a homesteader's wagon, but a salesman's wagon. The heat haze made estimating distances in the desert tricky, but he guessed another half an hour would bring him to the wagon—and its contents.

To cheer himself as he rode, he thought of all of the things he would do once he got to the next town. He'd stay at the best flophouse, maybe get a whore. And, of course, a gun. After the last few hours, he deserved it.

When he snapped out of his daydream, he was perhaps a half-mile behind the wagon. Through the dust its rickety wheels threw into the air, Gus could see the wagon was painted a bright red. Ornate woodwork covered its body, stenciled in gold and green.

A snake-oil man, Gus thought with pleasure. He'd be sure to have a whole heap of money.

As he drew along side the wagon, Gus saw the words "The Incredible Dr. Alatryx" painted onto it in tall, sky-blue letters. "Egypt, India, The Orient, Persia."

"Hello," said the driver, drawing the two horses in with a tug on the reins, and jumping from the front of the wagon. He was dressed in a dusty black suit, a black hat and polished snakeskin boots. Easterner, Gus snorted to himself. Gus noticed that the driver limped a bit, favoring his left foot as he walked toward him, hand outstretched.

Gus dismounted and took the man's gloved hand. "Pleased to meet you."

He grimaced at the man's limp handshake, took his hand back quickly.

"And I, friend, am pleased to meet you," the man said, removing his hat and wiping his forehead with an immaculate white silk handkerchief. "I'm Dr. Alatryx, and I am at your service." He made a deep bow, bending crisply at the waist. "How can I help?"

"Well, a drink'd be good."

Dr. Alatryx looked at him, and Gus noticed that his eyes were a strange reddish-violet. They were intense, giving his face an otherworldly cast, as if he *did* hold some mysterious power to cure what mortal doctors could not.

"Then, friend, we shall share what I have." He walked past Gus toward the back entrance of the wagon. His unworried, unafraid demeanor confounded Gus.

Dr. Alatryx inserted an ornate silver key into a lock on the wagon's rear door, drew it open with a low creak. He ducked into the wagon's dark recesses, and Gus heard the sound of many things being moved here and there inside.

The doctor reappeared with a bottle of amber fluid and two clear, crystal glasses. "Here we are," he said, handing a glass to Gus. He uncorked the bottle, poured a generous shot into Gus' glass, then his.

The label on the bottle read, "Dr. Alatryx's Mysterious Persian Cure. Good For ALL AILMENTS! Indigestion! Headaches! Tooth Pain! Gout! Piles!"

Gus didn't wait for the doctor to fill his own glass. The whiskey's fire cut through the dirt, dust and dryness. Saliva sprang inside his mouth like a gusher, following the whiskey down his throat. Gus moistened his lips with his newly wet tongue, and laughed a little at the "Mysterious Persian Cure" before taking another draught.

Dr. Alatryx watched Gus with amusement, then took a small drink from his own glass. "Where are you heading, friend?"

"Whatever town'll have me," Gus laughed, finished the whiskey in his glass. Dr. Alatryx refilled it for him. Gus stared into the whiskey as he swirled it.

"Trouble?"

Gus jerked his head up and looked at the doctor. "What business is that of yours?"

"None at all, friend. But if there were trouble, I have in my wagon things that could help you."

Gus took another drink, his eyes staring at Dr. Alatryx over the rim of the glass, his brow a map of frustration and interest. "What makes you think I'm in any trouble, stranger?"

"What makes a man ride through the desert in the middle of the day with no water, no hat?" he mused. "What makes a man flag down an ordinary patent-medicine salesman in the middle of said desert?

"What makes a man travel alone without a gun?"

Gus started. "What makes you think I don't have a gun?"

Dr. Alatryx laughed and set his glass of whiskey onto the step leading to the wagon's door. "A man like you would carry his gun for all to see. Since I see no gun, you must not have one." He leaned forward, dropped his voice to a conspiratorial whisper.

"Therefore, friend, you must need one."

Gus turned away from the doctor's gaze. His stolen bay cropped at a small clump of weeds it had found.

He didn't like the way the word *friend* spilled from this man's lips.

"'Spose I do need a gun? You got any?"

"Do I 'got' any?" he asked and laughed again. "Sir, Dr. Alatryx has been around the world. He has seen the mysteries of ancient Egypt. He has talked to the wizards of Persia. He has been privy to the secrets of the Orient. Just like the wagon says." He limped to the top step of the wagon, tapped its side and turned back to Gus. "You can read, can't you?"

"I can read," Gus said defensively. Dr. Alatryx disappeared again into the wagon. Gus leaned over to make sure he was preoccupied, then grabbed the bottle and filled his glass to the rim.

More sounds of things being moved, tossed and dragged around issued from the wagon's interior. "Yes, the Orient," came his voice. "Did you know that the Chinese invented gunpowder?"

Dr. Alatryx returned holding a wooden case. "The Chinese are a strange and wondrous people." He set the plain, polished wood box down on the wagon's last step and opened it. Inside, nestled in crushed red velvet, was a gun. Gus recognized it as a .44 caliber Remington No. 3. A six-shooter. Pretty good gun, though it had to be nearly seven years old.

The Remington's wooden grips had been replaced with grips of a dull black material that had strange carvings on them. On the case's opposite side was an impression in the velvet where a second gun had been.

"This is a special gun, the last of its kind," said Dr. Alatryx, drawing it reverently from its resting place. The black grips were highly polished, yet reflected little light.

"What's so special about a '75 Remington?" Gus asked. He was beginning to worry. This was taking too long. What if the posse was catching up with him? He knew Sheriff Holloran from previous encounters. He'd hang him out here from anything they could throw a rope over.

"Friend, this gun never misses."

"How's that?" asked Gus.

"This gun not only *never* misses, it *can't* miss. Do you hear what I'm saying, friend? It cannot miss. *Ever.*"

He handed the gun to Gus.

Gus turned the gun over in his hands. Other than the strange, carved grips, the gun looked like an ordinary Remington.

"Can't miss, huh?" asked Gus with aggravated disbelief.

"Correct."

Gus pointed the gun into the air. "So, if I wanted to shoot my horse, I could point the gun in the air and shoot, and the horse'd drop dead."

"Deader than a nail," said the doctor. His eyes were narrowed, and his mouth was drawn in a fierce smile. "But, friend, I should warn you…"

The gun went off with a crack, and Gus' arm jumped with the

kick of the first bullet.

From the front of the wagon came a loud whinny and the sound of a horse falling to the ground. Gus' smirk faltered, and he stood in shock for a moment.

Dr. Alatryx smiled, his perfect white teeth showing.

Gus sprinted to the front of the wagon and found the bay sprawled amidst the ragged plants it had been eating. There was a large hole through the back of its head, and blood beaded on the horse's smooth flanks.

It was, as Dr. Alatryx had predicted, deader than a nail.

Gus looked dumbly at the gun held in his hand. He had fired the gun into the air and had killed a horse standing more than 50 yards in front of him *on the ground*. As the implication of this seeped into his sun-baked brain, Dr. Alatryx came to stand beside him.

"You didn't let me finish. The gun's cylinder cannot be removed. The six bullets in the gun are the only six bullets it will ever fire. Well, I should say five now, though I suppose one bullet to prove its accuracy is one bullet well spent."

"How in the hell…? I mean, what kind of gun is this, anyhow?" sputtered Gus.

"As I said, friend, it is a special gun, the last of its kind. After its remaining five bullets are spent, there will be no more like it in the world," said the doctor.

"How much?" asked Gus, with no intention of buying it.

Dr. Alatryx drew a silver pocket watch out of his vest. He snapped it open. "Noon. Well, my friend, let's say we have a sale on this rare and potent weapon. For you, today, I'll sell it for $50."

Gus turned away and smiled, holding the gun pointed at the ground. The gun barked once, and the second bullet sped to its target.

Dr. Alatryx lay stretched on the ground. His hat had fallen off, and a spill of black hair swept the dust. A single red spot grew, spread along the whiteness of his shirt. His violet eyes remained open. Gus prodded him with his foot.

"Deader than a nail…and dumber, too," he laughed. He bent and pulled the silver watch from the doctor's dead hand. The thin chain holding it to his suit parted. Gus looked at the watch, stuffed it into his pocket.

He walked back to the rear of the wagon and picked up his drink. Draining it, he climbed the stairs and entered the wagon's cramped, hot interior.

Dr. Alatryx, as it happened, turned out to have everything Gus wanted. Everything, that is, except for the whore…and the gun's mate. He even searched Dr. Alatryx's body for the second gun. The doctor carried no weapon. Damn fool, thought Gus.

He dressed himself in a dark brown suit of fine material, just his size. He found a new brown bowler in a box under reams and reams of oriental-looking cloth. He found and took more than $500 in gold, hidden inexpertly in a leather bag behind a loose plank in the wagon's wall.

In thirty minutes, as his new watch told him, he stood outside the wagon again, swallowing another glass of the late doctor's miracle cure. He threw the empty glass into the desert and put the bottle into his saddlebag, which now hung from the back of one of the doctor's beautiful black stallions. It was, Gus mused, the prettiest horse he'd ever stolen.

He climbed into the saddle, the horse unaware or uncaring of the fact that he had shot its owner. He turned to look in the direction of the pursuing posse.

The cat's tail wagged a lot closer than it had the last time he checked.

Smiling, Gus drew the gun from its new holster on his hip, looked at it quizzically. He turned in the saddle, pointed the gun approximately in the direction of the cat's tail and fired.

"The devil take ya, Holloran!"

The horse, frightened by the noise, pranced nervously, upsetting his lazy aim. Another time, another place, another gun, Gus would have been angry at the animal. Now, he only laughed as he put his new spurs to the horse's sides and galloped away.

About seven miles west of Gus, the posse had paused so its nine members could drink from their canteens. A tall, bearded man took a long draught, wiped his mouth with the back of his sleeve.

"Gettin' closer boys. I expect we'll have him before dinner," said the man, capping his canteen and replacing it in his saddlebag. The other men, taking their lead from him, finished their drinks and repacked their canteens.

"In a couple miles, we'll split up. Mike, you, Jimmy and Matt'll go north. Me, Lou, Joe and…" The man grasped his chest, flipped violently backward in his saddle, tumbled to the ground behind his horse. The other men dismounted quickly, drew and cocked their guns, and approached him.

When they turned him over, they scanned the desert warily. For on Sheriff Timothy Holloran's chest, just below and to the right of his silver badge, another badge had appeared, red and wet and more meaningful than anything he had ever worn in his life.

Gus dismounted from the black horse, tied it to a railing in front of the Esmeralda Hotel in the small town of Gasping Gulch. The name fit, for Gus noticed that the town barely held back the desert. Dry tumbleweeds blew along the streets, and dust devils spun into existence, twirling away like phantom dancers.

He removed his saddlebag from the horse with some difficulty, his new-found property weighing it more than he was accustomed. He climbed the creaking steps to the Esmeralda, and pushed through its doors.

Several men looked up from card games, drinks, or women to see who had entered. Almost in unison, a wrinkle of disgust passed across their faces.

For a moment, Gus wondered at why he merited this sort of reception. Then, he realized. The clothes he was wearing. Everyone took him for an Easterner.

He walked through a side door in the bar and stopped at the

hotel's front desk. No one was there, so he rang the bell.

From the same door he entered came a man he assumed to be the owner of the hotel. "Yeah?" he asked. "What can I do for you, stranger?"

"I'd like a hot meal, your best room and your prettiest woman for the night. In that order."

The man looked at him with mild disgust. Gus reached into his pocket and drew out $50 in gold coins. He plunked them on the counter.

"I reckon this'll cover it."

The man picked up a coin, examined it. "I'll be damned. You'll get the best room, the best meal and the best girl, I'll see to that, mister. Just why are you in this godforsaken place anyway?" He slid the money into his waiting hands, deposited it into a pocket behind his apron.

"Just passing through," said Gus.

"Sure, I understand. Betty!" he yelled. A couple of seconds later an attractive, if worn, brunette woman walked through the door from the bar. She wore a short, frilly red dress, a garter on her thigh and a tattered feather in her hair.

"Yeah?" She eyed Gus from foot to crown.

"The gentleman here will be staying with us for a few days, and he'd like a friend. So, why don't you help him upstairs and be real friendly-like to him?"

"Sure," she said, sidling up to Gus and putting her arm through his. "What's your name?"

"Gus," he croaked. He smelled whiskey on her breath and smoke in her hair, but he was excited.

"Well, Gus, how'd you like for me to get you outta these fancy duds and give you a bath?" she asked, giggling as she led him up the stairs to his room.

Four-twenty five on the silver pocket watch.

Gus put himself back into his stolen clothes, adjusted them, looked at Betty sleeping in his bed. She'd been worth the money.

He strapped on his gun belt, drew the gun from its holster. The carvings deep in the black grips looked like foreign writing. Maybe German, Gus thought.

He closed the door softly, crept down the narrow corridor to the staircase, his new shoes creaking more than the dry floorboards.

In the bar, every head turned to him, as they'd done before. But this time, their faces wore expressions of interest, curiosity and, on some, avarice. Obviously, the innkeeper had been regaling them with talk of the new guest and his ready finances. Gus would have to be on guard against men wanting to take advantage of this situation—*men like him*.

Gus strode to an empty table and sat, all eyes on him. He looked around the room, and the innkeeper took this as a sign that he was needed.

"Yes, sir, can I help?"

"Yeah, I think I'll have me some dinner now," Gus replied. "Beefsteak, some potatoes, some bread and butter, and some pie, any kind'd be fine. Oh, and some whiskey, too. Best in the house."

"Of course," said the man. He leaned close to Gus, nudged him with an elbow. "Work up an appetite, huh?"

"Yeah, I guess you could say that."

The innkeeper came back with a whiskey bottle and a glass. In due course, the steak, a baked potato, a warm loaf of new bread, butter, and a half an apple pie followed. Gus pounced on the food, tucking pieces of steak in as quickly as he could chew and swallow. Everybody still watched, but what the hell, he thought. Let 'em.

He was comforted by the weight of the strange, cold gun strapped to his thigh.

He continued to cut, chew, drink and swallow until he had eaten it all. His head swam with the half-bottle of whiskey he had used to wash it all down. He pulled the pie tin to him and started on its contents.

As he pushed an aromatic fork-full of the apple pie into his mouth, however, a hand came down on his. It pulled the fork from his mouth and sent it clattering across the wooden floor.

"Whaa…," Gus mumbled around a mouthful of pie. He turned, half expecting to see Sheriff Holloran. His hand dropped to his gun belt.

"I wouldn't."

Gus stood, froze when he saw who it was.

He looked a little worse for wear, but it was him, right down to the piercing red-violet eyes. He wore a different hat and a long, tan oilskin coat that swung around his knees. One of his hands pushed the coat aside at waist level, then rested firmly on his hip to reveal a gun.

Oh, no. Oh, shit, no.

Carved deeply into its dull, black grips were a series of lines, shapes and seemingly meaningless squiggles.

"You're dead," was the only thing he could think of to say.

"I don't know what you're talking about," said Dr. Alatryx. He pulled out a seat, sat at the table. "Sit, friend, we have business to discuss."

Gus sat, looked around. People were watching, trying hard to pretend that they weren't. "Dressing and living well on my money, I see. Oh well, no matter. What's done is done, friend," the doctor said. But, this time the word *friend* was sneered. "There is, however, the small matter of payment."

"Okay. Fair is fair," whispered Gus. "I'll pay you a hundred and fifty dollars for the gun and everything."

"Do you take me for a fool? You stole the money from me along with everything else," laughed Dr. Alatryx. "No, what I want is something that you cannot welsh on. Something infinitely more valuable.

"You."

Gus blinked.

"What the hell's that mean?" he asked.

"Tomorrow at noon. Just you and me. We've each got one of the guns, so it depends merely on who is fastest."

"What if I say no?"

"Then, friend, I will shoot you where you sit with my last bullet."

"Tomorrow at noon?" asked Gus. "No funny business?"

"None. I give my word. Shake?" he asked, and he held out a gloved hand.

Gus took the doctor's limp hand in his with a grimace of distaste.

Dr. Alatryx stood. "I would get plenty of rest were I you." He turned and took two steps toward the bar's street exit. "Oh, and don't think about leaving town," he said turning back to Gus. "I've taken the liberty of shooting your—I mean *my*—horse. Good night."

And he left the bar.

Gus sat for a minute, stunned. He eyed the pie and realized his appetite had left him. In fact, he felt decidedly queasy. He stood and left the bar. When he got to his room, Betty was gone, but that was just as well. He slipped out of his clothes and got into bed. He placed the gun under his pillow and, surprisingly, went straight to sleep.

He awoke with the sun in his eyes. The white linen curtains flapped in the breeze from the open window. He swung his legs over the edge of the bed, sat for a few minutes. Standing, he walked to the chest of drawers near the door. A porcelain basin and a china pitcher sat on the chest. He poured some of the water from the pitcher into the basin and washed his face. The water was tepid and oily.

It was early, and it seemed as if the town had not yet risen. He thought about what he was going to do today: leave or stay another day or two and impress the locals. And risk capture.

Then he remembered what had happened last night, and he flopped onto the bed. He had a gunfight to attend this morning, and he could see no way of getting out of it.

Gus stared bleakly at the strange gun hanging in its belt from the back of a chair.

"Well, shit," he said aloud, jumping to his feet. "It don't matter none that my horse is dead. I've got money! I can buy another horse and get outta here!"

He clambered into his clothes, packed his belongings into his saddlebag, hefted it quietly into the hotel's corridor. He crept down the steps, past the front desk and into the bar. The innkeeper was busy cleaning, preparing for the day's business.

"Mornin'," he said when he saw Gus heading for the front door.

"Howdy," Gus said softly. "You reckon anyone in town is awake and can sell me a horse?"

The innkeeper looked at Gus with mild interest. "Sure, Billy down at the blacksmith's shop has a couple, and he's probably awake by now. You fixin' to leave?"

"That's right."

"I don't give no refunds."

"Keep the goddamned money," said Gus, turning toward the door and leaving the innkeeper to smile at his unexpected good fortune.

Once outside, he chose to walk on the dirt street rather than the plank sidewalks so as not to make noise and attract attention. Looking both ways along the street, he saw the blacksmith shop about four buildings to his right. He walked quickly toward it.

He came to the shop's big stable doors and was about to knock.

"Going somewhere, friend?"

Gus turned, and there he was...*again*. He no longer wore the coat that covered his gun belt; the holster rested empty against his hip. The gun was in his pale hand, the muzzle pointing unwaveringly at Gus.

"Just checkin' to see if there was a horse for sale...for after our business," Gus blurted.

Dr. Alatryx smiled. "Confidence is a charming quality. Overconfidence is a deadly one," he said. "Should we attend to our business, friend?"

Gus sighed and dropped his saddlebag to the ground. He frowned slightly and said yes, his hand dropping nonchalantly to the gun in his own holster.

Dr. Alatryx cocked his gun in warning.

Gus squeezed the trigger without taking his gun from its holster. As he pulled it, he heard Dr. Alatryx's gun click in front of him.

Jammed.

Gus' gun boomed, echoing across the wooden canyons of the town.

His fourth bullet crashed into a surprised Dr. Alatryx's chest, shoving him backwards, his arms pinwheeling, the gun torn from his hand. A gout of blood and gore splashed the dusty red wall of the blacksmith shop. Dr. Alatryx slumped against the wall and lay there.

Gus shook with the rush of fear that swept through his body.

"Shit," he whispered. He knelt near Dr. Alatryx and examined the wound. The son of a bitch had to be dead now. He stood and prodded the body with his foot.

Nothing.

He bent, lifted the gun Dr. Alatryx had dropped. He was careful to point it away from himself.

As if it mattered.

Dr. Alatryx's last bullet unjammed itself and roared from the barrel, lifting a thick patch of hair and scalp from the top of Gus' head, matted with whitish-red clots, and slapping it against the rough wooden wall near the doctor's bloodstain.

Gus' body stood for a moment as if not understanding that it was dead before collapsing in a heap next to the doctor.

Gus' stolen brown bowler bounced down the dusty street on its rim, joining a herd of desiccated tumbleweeds as they rolled out of town.

A bucket of water splashed against the wall, and the gore mixed with the dust to form a foul-colored paste. The sheriff, also the town's general store owner, hooked his arms under Gus' body, which hung limply from under the bed sheet the innkeeper had brought. A deputy took Gus' feet, and the two carried the body to the sheriff's office, where they laid it on a pallet inside one of the empty cells.

"Are you sure there's no other bodies?" asked the sheriff. "People are sayin' they heard two shots. And there were two stains on the wall. But that poor bastard's only got one wound. Not that it weren't enough."

"No, sir, I checked all over," the young deputy answered. The sheriff took the answer at face value, but knew he'd be spending the better part of his day searching the town anyway.

The office door rattled, and two men walked in. The sheriff caught a brief glimpse of a crowd.

Let'm wait. I'll show the body later.

The first man was the innkeeper. "Must be our lucky day," he said. "Sheriff, this here man's an undertaker makin' his way to California. He said he'd be glad to help."

The second man was dressed in black, a tall hat crowned his head, and two streamers of black crepe flowed down from the top of the silk hat and covered his face. A long coat protected his suit from the dust.

"Pleased to meet you, friend," said the undertaker, offering his hand to the sheriff, who took it and released it quickly, a glimmer of disgust crossing his features.

"Well, sir, seein' as how this man has plenty of money, we've got gold to pay you," said the sheriff as the undertaker bent, uncovered the body.

"Dead as a nail," clucked the undertaker.

He reached into Gus' vest, drew out the silver pocket watch. It opened with a snap, and he smiled. "This will be all the payment I require."

"Fine. There's a cemetery about two miles outside town," said the sheriff.

"When I finish my business, I will take him there. It's the least

I can do for my payment." The undertaker closed the watch, slipped it into his vest.

As the undertaker stood, the folds of his coat parted to reveal two black guns strapped across his hips, each with intricately carved ebony handles.

"That's the most heavily armed undertaker I've ever seen," whispered the sheriff to the innkeeper.

The innkeeper, however, was lost in thought, trying hard to remember exactly where he had seen a gun like those before.

BOOMER BOY, NOW YOU'RE A MAN

by Walter Giersbach

I swore I was as much of a man as any round this territory or in the town of Guthrie for I had shot a coyote and fought off a wildcat with nothing more than a stick, but my Pa just laughed. "You're a 16-year-old and you got a heap of living to do before you're growed up."

Well, much as I respect my old man he can go shit a pinecone. I had dreams and I was going to make them come true. Hadn't we—Pa and Ma and my two sisters—beat the Sooner land grabbers the year before, staked our claim to 160 acres of Oklahoma Territory and cleared the land?

We were honest Boomers of 1889. Fact is, Pa and me had even put a few shots over the heads of some claim jumpers. Like to think I winged one, but I don't know. And we needed a keen eye for the Cherokee and Creeks lurking about wanting to steal our chickens and the cow and horse.

"It's not easy work, Christopher," Pa always told me to the point of exasperation. "Good things don't come easy."

"I ain't bragging. Just saying I do my day's chores from sunup to sundown. Every day is hot and dry as Hades with the dusty sun in my eyes. And we need another pair of eyes just to see who or what might be creeping up on us as we get ready for planting."

My Pa is a good and honest man. But what I mean to say is that I had dreams of leaving this all behind and becoming a writer, one of the very best kind who wrote those dime novels I bought (when my folks weren't looking) on our trips into Guthrie. My hero was Ned Buntline, who did that story about Wild Bill Hickok's life and even knew Buffalo Bill Cody. Hadn't he also commissioned a .45 single action Colt with a 12-inch barrel known as the Buntline Special? The notable lawmen Bat Masterson and Wyatt Earp even carried a Special.

"Soon as we have time, maybe when winter comes," I confessed to Pa, "I will put pen to paper and see if the Guthrie newspaper would print a tale or two."

Well, sir, I believe it was a day in June and dry as a boar's tit that I was digging post holes when I jerked around hearing a noise. This Indian woman—girl, I figured in a moment—stood up and she had my water jug.

"Hey, you let go my water," I shouted and raised my shovel.

"No, please, just some water," she said, speaking English good as any school marm.

"Well, you best ask first, missy. Not just steal a man's water." But I seen that she was prettier than the Indians I saw in Guthrie and not anything to be feared of. "What's your name?"

"My name is Ahyoka. It means She Brought Happiness."

"Well, I am Chris Walker and it don't mean anything except my Pa is George Walker."

"Quiss?"

"No, can't you say Chris? *Crrr-isss.*" I didn't know then that Cherokees can't pronounce the letters CR.

"Quiss." She smiled the prettiest smile I'd seen since we left Illinois.

Oh, Ahyoka, Ahyoka, Ahyoka, that was the beginning of a new life for me. Pa would be working on the irrigation system down at the stream and had me doing more post holes and fencing. Ahyoka would come to me with some corn dodgers or dried meat and we would talk about her life and the life I left behind. And one day to my great surprise she kissed me. On the mouth, and said I was a good man. Did you hear? She called me a man. She knew what I meant when I said I was going to be a writer of brave tales, for she had learned the Cherokee writing system that she called *asgaya gigageyi*. "I hope to become a teacher, of the children of my people. All children."

"And I, a writer of exciting tales to amuse and entertain and educate."

There were many summer days that Ahyoka and I met in the fields or under the trees, and many tender kisses. Then she introduced me to the language I only read about in the Bible's Song of Solomon, "Let him kiss me with the kisses of his mouth! For your love is better than wine." I had looked that up to memorize it.

I told Ahyoka, "I compare you, my love, to a mare among Pharaoh's chariots. Your cheeks are lovely with ornaments, your neck with strings of jewels."

"You think I am a horse?" And she laughed. I laughed too, because I realized she had captured my heart.

Screwing up my courage for fear of my family's disapproval, I took Ahyoka to our house and introduced her. Ma said, "She is sweet, Chris. A fine woman, even though an Indian." And Pa, who had met many more Cherokee, talked at length with her about the past tribulations of her people and of the future. I know they both disapproved of the Indians as uncivilized creatures, but they were being charitable while Ahyoka was in our house.

But one day Ahyoka failed to appear, and also for many days later. I was sorely worried and told Pa I needed to go to her home and ask after her. Her father was Degotoga, which Ahyoka said means Standing Together. He was a farmer, like Pa, but on a poorer and smaller scale. Worse, he had been digging a well for more water and at 36 feet down black rock oil began pouring out to his great anger.

Degotoga, whom I had never met, was quiet in welcoming us. "The one who filled my days with happiness no longer walks this earth," he said, sitting in the dirt in front of his house. "She will no longer greet the day with a smile. She will no longer sing songs."

"What do you mean?" I asked.

"Ahyoka is dead." He spit out the unspeakable facts quickly. "When she did not return to prepare the evening meal, I went to search. She was killed and left by the road into Guthrie.

"No one can tell me what happened. I heard talk there were men about a mile to the south, drinking and shouting about killing Indians. One said he had killed an Indian just outside of town. I thought the worst and went to search. When I got there, the men were gone. I found my daughter's body under a pinyon tree. She was killed, her breasts cut off, her body torn apart, and then left by the road."

He went back to chanting to the Creator, in English and Cherokee, asking him to put a curse on the killer, that he may suffer the same pain a thousand times over.

Walking home, Pa told me to forget my friend. "Listen to me because I'm wiser," he said. "After her burial, the medicine man told the others to speak her name no more. This will make sure Ahyoka will find her way to the other world and not be called back to this one."

But I swore at that moment I would put a bullet through the heart of the miscreant who had killed my love, and I went home that night and cried.

Oklahoma was hard and unyielding to our plow, watered by the drying stream and the never-ending wind that blew over the prairie. I cursed the land, which was drying me up inside too.

Not long afterwards, Pa said, "Son, I can work the farm with your sisters and Ma. I know you are not happy. You go to Mr. Deutsch at the newspaper and see if he will take you on as a reporter if that is where your heart is. I can see you don't want to be a farmer like me, like your grandpa."

So I did and thus my career was born at the *News Leader*, a paper that was but one year old and served our community well, as rough a town as ever there was.

I was no more than a few months at the newspaper when I

was having a beer and some lunch at the Branding Iron Saloon when I overheard a loud fellow exclaiming about the Indians.

"You sure got them pegged, Thomas," said a man I saw as a trader or drummer.

"Them fucking Indians better watch it around white Christian men."

"What a strange tobacco pouch you carry," said the trader. "It looks like a woman's breast."

"It's a squaw's tit she won't be needing anymore."

I got up from the bar and went over to the man, who was perhaps a few years older than me, but raggedy-looking and not pleasant at all.

"Did you happen to kill this young woman?" I asked.

"And what business is it of yours, pipsqueak?"

"Because I think you killed the woman I loved. Back a few months ago on the road to Guthrie."

"Fuck you, squirt."

Enraged by this uncivilized behavior I made a sudden movement. He responded by reaching into his belt where there was a large revolver. Quick as anything, I pulled my sheath knife out as the pistol emerged. When he pointed it at me, I plunged my blade into his heart.

"You have stabbed me!" he shouted.

I didn't know what I had done, for my action was neither Christian or well-considered. And then the plug ugly fell backward, knocking over his chair.

"That shall be your lesson for all eternity," I said to the dead man, for that is what he was. Dead. The trader simply looked at me, drank some of his beer, and said, "Fair is fair, I guess."

A Federal marshal happened through town some days later and sat me down in Mr. Deutsch's office. "The word is that you killed a man who was engaged in his noontime repast."

"I killed a killer, the murderer of my lady friend. And this is her body part he was using to hold tobacco." I flung Ahyoka's breast down on the desk.

"Well, young sir, there will be no charges. His companion said he was pulling his pistol as you stabbed him. A knife is usually no match for a gun, but I think you have done the right thing."

I reflected that I had done the proper thing by avenging Ahyoka's death, assuaging Degotoga's grief somewhat, and sealing my position as a man to be reckoned with in the new territory. Also, it became the first dramatic story I sold to *True Western Adventures*.

Mr. Ned Buntline sent me a letter asking for an interview, but he never answered my reply. We might have had a good talk, man to man.

HAVE TiME MACHiNE, WiLL TRAVEL

by Harri B. Cradoc

Light Commander LeGuin of the admiralty's Special Forces trained her weapon on the man who was trying on the cowboy outfit and pretended to fire. "Bang, you're dead."

Her target was still fingering the sweatband on his Stetson so it wouldn't crimp his ears. He gave up for the moment and just tucked it under his arm. "You're kidding, right?"

"Not a bit. If I had really fired you would have been thrown backwards with a hole in you the size of an ionic flow regulator." She rubbed the barrel of the Colt Peacemaker and admired it as if stroking the fur of a beautiful but wild animal. Then she held the gun out to Major Vernier and motioned for him to come get it. "This weapon killed a lot of bad guys in the Old West, and it would have made a nice dent in you, love."

Major Vernier approached the older officer and was not surprised when she took the opportunity to rub his crew-cut hair the way she had rubbed his gun. Then she spoke to him in a more confidential tone. "I'm glad they sent me someone of equivalent rank. I don't feel I have to ride your butt like you're fresh out of tactical school."

Then LeGuin shoved him away from her and headed for the saloon door. Dusty sunlight poked through the swinging slats onto the barroom floor, and a warm prairie smell was sweeping through the town. If it had been a real town, and a real prairie, a dozen cowhands would have whistled at the tight fitting jumpsuit and the weapon-toting woman inside.

"Can I have the bullets now?" asked Vernier.

"Not till I'm sure you know where to aim them," she called back through the long auburn hair that fell across her shoulder when she turned around.

"I've been practicing in the simulator aboard ship for a week."

LeGuin focused her hazel-fire eyes on him. "But this is real dirt blowing up your nostrils, not a bunch of artificially excited photons. This is different from a climate controlled simulator where you can take a bathroom break anytime you want."

"The buildings are fakes," said Vernier, pounding his fist on a shaky wall that was labeled Barber Shop and Dentistry. A hollow glass cylinder spun nearby with red and white stripes that went spiraling when he slapped them. "There's nothing behind the storefronts, except a few half-finished rooms. What did you call this?"

"A back lot, where movies were made. Did you study the ones I sent you?"

"Like my life depended on it." He grinned.

"Don't laugh," she said. "You're bound to make mistakes in a different time period, with an alien culture. The trans-mentor you're wearing can make you sound like an Earthling, but it can't make you act like one." She pulled five cartridges from her pocket and tossed them over.

"Hey," he mumbled, "it's not like it's my first rodeo."

When Vernier finished loading, he looked up to see LeGuin lining up drinking glasses that she must have pulled from her equipment bag or a part of her jumpsuit that he hadn't been studying as they walked. When she had a neat little row across a railing outside the barbershop, she turned and nodded to him. "Okay, lover boy, let's see how dangerous you can be."

She stepped back and folded her slender arms into her equally slender waist, and posed there for him like one of the women in the recruiting posters that had made him join the war effort in the first place. She was better looking than any of the models they had used, he thought, and stronger. She had thrown him across the simulation room several times while they were practicing hand-to-hand combat, and then she had proven how interesting she could be by giving him a rubdown after the exercise. When her hands got a grip on him, she was inescapable.

"What do you call this thing again?"

"A six-shooter," she said, "but it has only five bullets in it."

"So every sixth bad guy goes free?"

She sneered. "No. It's so you don't shoot yourself in the foot. Anyway, the only man who might stand up to you is our deserter, Colonels Wells."

"So he might shoot me?"

She smiled. "He might, but Wells knows he can't kill you with one of these things. Your skin will fold in around the bullet and you can just pull it out later. Now would you mind shooting some shot glasses for me?"

Vernier drew the ancient firearm and tried to imagine that it was pointing at a man instead of a set of glassware. It was not the same as pointing a stun gun with holographic sighting. It was more like spray painting a fence in a light breeze.

His first shots had left their targets still standing, as if the bullets had passed through a time displacement mechanism. But he knew the deserter had taken no fancy equipment with him. He was no more dangerous than these pieces of glass in front of him.

"No recoil in the simulator," said LeGuin, squinting at him.

More shots echoed off the vacant shops. Then the only sound was the light commander's boots scraping along the street. She replaced some glasses and said, "Try to anticipate the kickback, and compensate."

Vernier studied the light commander and the way the wind played in her hair.

"Suppose I find Wells, and he won't come back?"

"I need him alive," said the light commander. "He knows our

communications system, and since the radiation sickness has taken most of the crew, I have no one to replace him. Find out what's wrong in that brilliant brain of his, and convince him that he is needed."

"And if I can't?"

LeGuin's eyes remained as steady as if she were about to lay hands on him and embrace him. If she were closer he might reach out and squeeze an arm or two. One last fling for the road. She couldn't blame him for that.

"Then you must kill him," said the light commander. "He is too valuable to fall under enemy control. They may have agents looking for him even now."

Vernier squeezed off his shots and nodded at the result. There were no glasses standing on the wooden rail, only shards of glass buried in the yellow dirt as if sent there to draw blood from the ground.

"You've got a chance," said LeGuin, admiring his handiwork. Then she turned and strolled past him, avoiding any near contact, and not looking back.

They dropped him from orbit so he could see some of the terrain on the way down, but for the first minute, he was more interested in watching the silver hull of the mother ship as it pulled ahead of his single-passenger cocoon. The descent was slow at first, so Vernier got a good look at the bay doors that were closing above him, and he passed along the entire bottom half of the ship as he fell behind. The hull above him was pock-marked with small meteorite hits and blackened in several places from weapons fire. Normally the engineers would have fixed any battle damage in a matter of days. It had been a month since they last saw combat, so Vernier knew something was wrong. Either they had run out of repair kits for the engineers, or run out of engineers.

With a strange knot in his stomach, Vernier realized the

situation was more desperate than LeGuin had led him to believe. It was possible that she needed Wells, but not for the reason she stated. He might be useful in combat, but he might also be the only one left who could get their ship safely home.

If LeGuin needed Wells just to get the ship back home, then she was lying to the crew about their chances. Vernier realized she might have been lying to him, too. He had to wonder how much of the mission was still doable.

The cocoon shook rapidly, and gauges began to glow. A low hum filled Vernier's ears and then died away when he crossed the barrier. Half asleep, Vernier imagined LeGuin kissing him, and his daydream gave him a warm feeling long before the desert air danced over the cockpit door and slapped him in the face.

The one thing the newcomer could have used was a horse, but he was glad his equippers hadn't tried to fake one with a bunch of robotic parts. Instead, Vernier had been visually inspected by the history robot before he left, and that meticulous machine had pronounced him fit to saddle up, even if there was no horse to saddle up on.

Vernier lugged everything out of the cocoon and then punched the button that would activate the stealth wrap. The ship's outer skin shimmered for a second before reappearing in the same shape and color as the rocks around it. Vernier tapped on the rock where the cocoon's portal would be and he heard the hollow sound of an empty chamber behind it. "Don't forget to close the windows," he said. "It looks like rain."

The town could be seen down in a valley that Vernier approached by climbing over some large rocks. Some of them were big enough to be spaceships like his own, but none of them made hollow sounds when he kicked them with his hiking boots, so they were probably just rocks. Most of them, anyway.

After the rocks, a gently sloping field of grass led down to a small river and the wooden clapboard buildings that fronted the near side of a waterway. No one had built a bridge to the other side yet, so Vernier thought this must be a recent settlement, which was a good thing. Then everyone was a newcomer, and he might just fit in.

Soon a sign announced "Entering Sawmill River," in large burnt lettering. Underneath were letters that read "Population 154." Vernier wondered if he would be there long enough for someone to nail a numeral five over the four.

The sun was hot enough and the trail had been dry enough that Vernier thought he would investigate the nearest watering hole. That was the term the mission computer had used to mean a place where drinks were served.

One of the larger buildings in town had wagons hitched to a railing. One of the wagons had several uniformed men in it. Some wore blue pants with gold stripes down the side and matching neckerchiefs under hats folded up on one side. Four other men with long straight hair wore short scabbards that might have held knives.

Vernier lugged his saddlebags up three plank steps to the front door of the Sawmill Saloon and Boarding House, and pushed open the swinging doors.

The light inside was by oil lamp, which meant no electric power nearby. When he found an empty table in the corner, he pulled out his EMF detector, just to be sure. It was disguised as a case for gun shells and powder, in case he wanted to pack his own.

The dials of the detector could not be seen by anyone else in the Sawmill Saloon, because Vernier put his back to the wall and set a lumpy canvas bag on the table. Still, he watched the other patrons to make sure no one was paying too much attention to him. Of the dozen or so men who were standing at the bar, no one was even looking in his direction. Noises came from a back room, like dishes being cleaned, and footsteps came and went along a balcony above where doors hid other rooms. Bottles clanged against glasses on the bar, and silver coins jingled next to the drinks. Smoke rose from cigars stuck in metal ashtrays, only occasionally disturbed.

The men talked in murmurs that Vernier's equipment could not isolate, but he caught a few phrases like, "too hot to work," and "a log caught my hand." Nothing about strangers coming out of the hills, or odd lights in the sky, so Vernier relaxed. He went up to the bar and watched how the other men ordered drinks, then copied them. "Rye with a little water," he thought, pausing to make sure his trans-mentor had changed the idea into alien words.

One of the men near him spoke up. "Could be it's got a mite bit of water in it already."

The bartender laughed and slapped a glass down so that a reddish liquid in it sloshed onto the bar. He wiped up the spill with a damp towel. "Sorry. Some of us have forgotten our manners." Then he turned to wipe someone else's spill.

When Vernier turned around there was another man at his table, admiring the closed cover of the Colt Peacemaker box which hid the EMF signal detector. Of course, Vernier had thought to latch it before he left for his drink.

"A fine weapon," the man said when Vernier approached. The fellow nodded at the polished wooden handle stuck in Vernier's belt. "Shall we compare yours with mine?"

The man at the table seemed innocent enough. He wore mostly blue, like the men outside, but without any of the fringe, and his neckerchief hid his neck. He had dark hair and a mustache, and his chin needed a shave. He was holding out a Colt that looked exactly like Vernier's.

Not wishing to cause trouble, Vernier sat down and took the other man's gun to study it while sipping his drink. He felt a burning in his throat that told him why the local custom was to water down the drinks. A moment later, the stranger's voice said, "You don't mind, do you?"

"Oh, no," said Vernier, handing his gun to the man across the table. The other man inspected it briefly, even held it up to his nose for a moment, and then set it down on the table. Vernier did the same with his, noting how similar they were, and then returned his own gun to where it belonged.

"Hard to tell them apart, isn't it?" said the other.

"I don't know," said Vernier. "Mine's in my holster. That's how I know it's mine."

"Funny," said the other. "My name's McKie. The boys call me Sarge, because I'm kind of in charge of them, you see. Not real Army men, any of us, but the real soldiers let us wear some of their clothes so we recognize each other. We work out of the post just out of town. You probably saw some of my expert translators outside."

"Native Americans. Yes, I saw them on my way in."

McKie was looking down at the saddlebags on the floor. "If you don't mind my asking, where's your horse?"

"Had to leave him." That seemed non-committal enough, but it was the last of his pre-programmed answers.

"Did you shoot him with that gun you showed me?"

"Why do you ask?"

McKie smiled. "Because it didn't smell like it had been fired, and there were five bullets in the chamber." He went on smiling. "So you must reload every time you shoot a horse."

Vernier grinned back. "I didn't say I shot him."

"Buried him, though? You didn't leave him out for the buzzards, did you?"

Vernier decided to play along. No one on this planet was going to toy with him and get away with it. He reached down into his canvas bag and pulled out his fleet-issued collapsible shovel. He pressed a button on the side of its handle and a longer tube slid out to make a usable instrument about three feet long. He let McKie study it for a moment before pressing the button again and hiding the tool in his bag.

"Impressive," said McKie. "But you know the horse may have had the colic and fallen asleep. It might not have died if you kept it standing up a while."

"Is that right?"

"Yes, and as long as we're spraying horse-talk, yours might have got tired of you kicking him with those shiny boots you're wearing. Must be hard to keep your feet in stirrups with those."

Then Vernier remembered his spotlessly clean boots, never worn anywhere except in the sterile simulation room.

"You don't know much about horses, do you?" said McKie, laughing. "If they gave you one, you probably would have buried it alive. Except that ultra-light shovel doesn't have any dirt on it. Then there's your carrying case that makes your shirt glow. No, I don't need to see any more make-believe cowboy equipment."

Vernier swallowed some more of the horrible liquid in his glass and mumbled something that he hoped only one other set of ears would hear. "So it's not really Sergeant, is it?"

McKie glanced around casually. No one was paying the least bit of attention to the two phony westerners. When he seemed satisfied, he lifted his eyes briefly and said, "I was a light colonel up there. But going by Sarge does just fine down here. What's your pay scale, if you don't mind my asking?"

"It's Major. I am Major Jay Vernier. If I live another three or four days they might make me a colonel like you. Can't say how likely that is at this moment."

McKie leaned in. "We're all equals now. Just think of me as one of your best friends, and I might be your only friend, at that."

Vernier thought that a few adjustments to the plan were in order. He did some quick mental work on it and then said, "There's another ship, isn't there?"

McKie nodded and stroked his little mustache. "Yes, there is. You're sharper than you look in that comedian's outfit."

"Just out of curiosity," said Vernier, finishing his drink with a gulp, "when exactly did you spot me?"

"As you were coming in the saloon and before the doors swung shut behind you. I've never seen anyone wear spurs upside down before. Other than that, you look fine."

Vernier stood up. "That's very comforting. But I'm looking for a man named Wells."

McKie stood and took Vernier by the shoulder. "This is your lucky day. I am the one man in town who can take you to Wells. I'm ready if you are."

Vernier picked up his bags and shrugged them over his shoulders. "I guess I need all the friends I can get, and a couple of scouts and interpreters if you have them."

"Waiting outside in the buckboard," said McKie with a wave of his hand. "We are here to help you get that promotion."

They walked outside together, as if they were old pals. A man in the wagon saw McKie coming and untied the horses. In a minute the wagon was rolling down the main street of Sawmill River with Vernier taking it all in from the front seat. The man called Sarge snapped the reins lightly and the wagon picked up speed, even as the road got rougher.

One of the men riding in the back called up to Vernier, saying "Maybe you did not expect to be recognized. It is a wonderful thing, yes?"

"Yes," Vernier shouted back over the bouncing of the unsprung wheels. "I am quite happy to meet all of you."

One of the other men with long black hair and dark skin answered for the others. He tipped his hat toward Vernier and said in a loud voice, "Surprise!"

The trail along the river seemed like several hours, but no one in the wagon was checking any kind of timepiece. The men in the back pointed up to the sky and made comments in a language that Vernier could not understand. The trans-mentor device was slower than he had hoped, indicating a need for further sampling.

The wagon climbed with the river and the types of trees changed with the altitude, until only the hardiest of fir trees were left. The sky above them opened up and became an ocean that poured out on the far horizon. As the sun dropped, a mountain pass rose up to meet it and Sarge pointed in that direction. "The sides of that canyon are too steep for our wheels. We'll have to get out soon."

"And walk?" said the passenger.

"No," Sarge laughed, "but you could swim."

Vernier stared ahead as they went into the pass and finally he saw a shack and a dock beyond which a boat was tied at the edge of a river. The wagon stopped when it came even with the shack and two of the men stayed with the horses. Sarge led Vernier and the other two men to the dock and half-guided, half-pulled Vernier into the boat with him. Sarge gave him a long pole and told him to sit in the front and keep on the lookout.

"For what?" said the man with the pole.

"Logs," said the other. "I wouldn't want any of the big ones to hit us and send us to the bottom."

"The bottom of what?" asked the newly appointed lookout.

"Sky Lake," said Sarge. "It gets its color from the rocky shoreline and an endless supply of clouds from the north. No logger would come up this far, and not many visitors make it here either."

"How many is 'not many'?"

Sarge muttered, "You're the first."

When the boat reached the far shore of Sky Lake, Vernier stepped out and tried to adjust to solid ground again. After traveling in space, a ride on a river didn't seem like much, but he found it took him a minute to get his bearings. During this time he spotted a group of women coming down from a cluster of wood and thatch buildings up the slope. They were dressed, not in any military fashion, but more as the native population.

Vernier looked around. The soldiers near him were like the men who had rowed the boat. They were all of reddish brown skin and had long black hair tied behind their heads or tucked into their caps. Only he and Sarge had complexions bleached by artificial light. "Where are the others?" was all Vernier could think to say.

"You mean the crew? Some of them are still here, in a way. If I told you exactly what happened, it might scare you off."

"I have a psychological profile," said Vernier, without revealing anything another officer would not already know. "My tendencies are thoroughly screened before any mission."

"I'm sure," said the other. "And your vulnerabilities would be known as well."

They walked to meet the women with the smock-like dresses that did not stir much as they moved. When they were just a short distance away, Vernier could see that the seams of the dresses were decorated with silver thread and gemstones that glittered in the sun.

"Come with us," the middle one of the three said. Vernier stepped forward but stopped when he realized he was alone.

"They'll take you the rest of the way," said Sarge. "Pleasant journey!"

Vernier felt a tug and was soon being pulled up the hill with one of the female guides on either arm and the third leading the way. A trail opened between some mountain firs, and the women picked up their pace as they sensed their young charge could keep up with them. An hour of climbing followed, and then they stopped at the side of a cliff where the trail veered off as if to circle around another way.

"What's this?" Vernier asked. The women on either side of him stepped back and the guide in front stretched her hand toward the cliff face.

"He is waiting," said the woman. She produced a shiny box from a pocket in her dress and pointed it in the general direction of a large rock to her right. The rock shimmered briefly and changed in shape and color. Then it was a door.

In a moment Vernier was standing on a rounded ledge, like a platform, high above a sunlit oval of grass about three hundred feet wide. In the center, glowing in the mid-afternoon sun, was a large metal object with stubby wings and ribbed portals where two of the admiralty's finest engines were purring and making the air vibrate with the barest hint of their power.

The main hatch lay open and a gangway had been lowered into the flowing grass. A slight breeze, no doubt caused by a tuning cycle of the engines, left a slight ring in Vernier's ears as he climbed into the ship. The ringing went away as he entered the control room and there was only a faint hum from the floor panels as he stepped closer to the center of the room. Through various hatches in the control room walls it was possible to see into other areas of the ship. They were all well-lit and apparently powered up. Figures went back and forth between Vernier and the other sources of light, but none of them stopped to notice him. They might be members of the original crew, or they could be more ersatz soldiers with knives in their belts.

Speculation was put to an end by the swiveling motion of the main control chair. A man sitting there raised one hand in greeting. In the other hand was an officer's pellet blaster, not as large as a Colt Peacemaker, but just as deadly.

"If you've come in peace, I'll put this away," said the man pointing the blaster.

"Peaceful enough. I'm alone at any rate. How dangerous could I be?"

"Right you are. Unless you've come to kill me."

"Why would I do that?"

"Oh, lots of reasons come to mind: running from a fight, deserting Commander LeGuin in her hour of need, stealing one of the admiralty's cruisers. I suppose you could have been told to kill me for any one of those reasons."

Vernier said, "I was sent to talk to you."

"Talk, that's all? Are you sure you weren't sent to fly this ship home or put me in cuffs?"

"Quite sure," said Vernier, pulling his Colt out by two fingertips. The man in the chair watched as the barrel was spun and five bullets dropped into an open palm. "There you go. If I wanted to kill you, I would have to reload the gun, and you'd have plenty of time to blast or stun me before I did."

"I'll keep that in mind. I go by Harrison Griswold Wells, now. Sounds more like a local. My men and I are the new owners of this spacecraft. Repairs are underway and we will be leaving soon." The colonel stood and pocketed his weapon. He was tall, gaunt, and had a chiseled look to him. His face no longer had the pale tones of a space traveler, but was tanned and creased by the alien sun. He was like the native soldiers with their strong and healthy look. He had adapted quickly.

The tall man extended a hand in greeting and Vernier took it, saying "I've never shaken hands with a full colonel before."

"We've dispensed with the more inconvenient formalities. You'll get used to it."

"This is still business," said Vernier coldly. "It's even more serious if you have, as you say, stolen a spaceship."

"Oh, that? Well, I was just being self-critical there. It is part of my profile, you know, but I am a full colonel and entitled to indulge my whims, one of which is to fix this flagship and get it back in the sky without any interference from the outside."

"And by interference, you mean the people on my ship who are looking for you?"

The colonel's eyes narrowed and studied Vernier for any telltale signs of uneasiness that might indicate deception. Vernier hoped there were no such signs, as he had been honest so far and stated his business as plainly as possible.

"I mean your ship is disabled," said Wells, "and you can't go back home without spare parts that are only available here, from me."

Wells moved to one of the open bulkhead doors that framed the flickering light. The clattering of heavy equipment came from all corners of a compartment that was the hangar deck. Sparks flew where men were welding, and here and there a robot was lifting panels and placing them against some hollow framework.

"It's all here," said Wells when they reached a vantage point from which the entire deck could be seen. "You recognize that device over there?

"Looks like a star engine. And over there a cruiser's main blaster. It looks like you have all the spare parts that a fleet would need, if we had a fleet."

Wells drew a breath of the spark-tinged air. "We could have a fleet again, if LeGuin stays off my back long enough. I have the means to make a dozen ships. We're smack atop mineral heaven here. Rebuilding the admiralty's power with this as a base is not only possible, it would be easy. You can see I'm doing it."

Vernier estimated at least twenty men and women were working in the hangar. They all had the reddish brown skin and black hair of the soldiers. That gave Vernier a sinking feeling.

"Where are the others?" he asked.

"This is my crew now," said Wells. "Where is yours? I know most of them are dead. Many of the rest are dying from radiation or battle injuries. When you ask me how many are left of my crew, you should ask yourself how many of your own will be left in a year."

"So this is your answer? You train native people on another planet to build and maintain star engines they have never seen before?"

Wells took Vernier by the shoulders. "These people are smart and not afraid to work. When I taught them our language, they laughed. Their everyday speech is more complicated and colorful than ours, containing metaphors we hear only in poetry. I taught them to talk like full-fledged engine techs in no time."

Vernier cringed at the obvious message. "You are their leader now?"

"I lead this small group, yes. They were warriors, soldiers of a kind, but their weapons were taken away by the regular army that came from the East. You probably met some of those men, the ones in the blue suits?"

"Your men dress almost the same way."

"You can believe what LeGuin told you, or you can see for yourself. I didn't come here to judge these people. I came because we were running from an enemy that was defeating us at every turn. We needed a place to regroup and rebuild. I have found such a place. Magnetic qualities in the rock formations can keep us hidden for a hundred years."

Vernier had doubts. "What did you promise them?"

Wells was ready for that. "They are being driven out of their ancestral land and told to relocate. I have offered them a way to become strong again."

"Using star engines and blaster guns? The thought makes me nervous."

"I doubt that," said Wells. "Your profile is one of utter calm and level thought patterns. But we should move on. My personal library is just beyond this door."

The library had actual books and other artifacts found on various planets. It was well insulated from the noise outside, and had two comfortable chairs. Wells sat in one of them, while Vernier looked around, eventually speaking first. "Where do our other ships fit in?"

"Do you know of any?" asked Wells. "Perhaps LeGuin has not told you. We are virtually alone."

"Or some could be hiding, just like you."

"The main problem," said Wells, "is that LeGuin has not agreed to combine forces. She wishes to remain independent."

Vernier bit his lip. "You mean she thinks you're a renegade, out of control, and too dangerous to deal with?"

"My profile," said Wells, "is of one who takes chances, and I will take one now. I propose that you take over for me. When I am too old to do this anymore, there must be a younger man who knows the fleet and what we're fighting for."

"What we once fought for," corrected Vernier. "We haven't been in shape to do any fighting for several months, in case your spy equipment hasn't told you that."

"That can change," said the colonel. "You can change it. You've seen the progress we've made here. Think about my offer, but not as long as you usually do." Wells shrugged. "That's in your file, too."

Vernier had trouble imagining himself as a commander. "What about your second, McKie? He is between you and me in age."

"Didn't you notice the radiation burns on his neck? He's got less time than I do, and we're all that's left. Sorry, son, but I'm afraid you're it."

Vernier shook his head.

"Let me go back. I need to talk to LeGuin."

Wells was pleased. "Someday the other side of this mountain will have a ghost town, much like the one used for your training sessions. I can get you there almost immediately."

A short time later, Vernier was back in his own time. Presumably, he could now be seen from any ship orbiting the planet, and was already registering on LeGuin's sensor panel.

Liquor shimmered in one bottle behind the bar. Vernier grabbed it and poured some into a tin cup, and then offered a toast to the man in the mirror: "To places we'll never see again." He sat down on a stool, took off his hat, and waited.

The only cowboy in town had barely finished his drink when he heard the whirring of another cocoon as it landed in the street outside. The saloon doors were pushed open just as Vernier banged his cup down, and the newcomer's eyes were attracted by the sound. "So you're back!" she said. Then the light commander crossed the barroom floor and gave Vernier a hug.

"I'm afraid I may have lost the ship you sent me in. I had to leave it back in the last time period, or whatever they call them around here."

"Centuries," she said, rubbing her hand across the hair on his head. There might have been a little sweat mixed in with the bristles, but she didn't seem to mind. "You must have found Colonel Wells, but he wasn't the one who brought you."

"Right. He's back there, hiding out. He's got a ship and a crew, but it's not any crew of ours. He's using native people. They found a large ship and salvaged it."

"Interesting." said LeGuin. "Can this ship fly?"

"My guess is not yet, but pretty soon, in their time. His recruits are quick learners, and they're just as eager as he is to get away. They're being chased by an army with superior weapons as part of an expansionist move."

LeGuin blew some dust off the bar in front of her. "It never changes," she said. "You get a chance to disable anything?"

"Wells never let me go anywhere without him, and he had men crawling over every vital piece of machinery. I can go back and try to sneak aboard, if that's what you want."

"No, it's better that you don't. If this ship made it through a time shift, it must be in better shape than ours. What we need is to commandeer this other ship. Did Wells say he was staying or leaving?"

"He wants to give his natives a chance to resettle somewhere else. They don't care where they go, as long as it's far away from here."

LeGuin sat down on the stool next to Vernier. "Pour me some of whatever you're drinking." But a sudden whirring noise made her put down her cup. "That would be our deserter, if I've timed it right."

Vernier edged toward the windows, some of which were broken and gave a clear view of the street. "What sort of timing have you done? Does he know you're here?"

"He couldn't know," LeGuin said with a smirk. "I waited until he was in transit, so his sensors were down. He's using you to get to me. He'll try to talk you into killing me, if he hasn't already. He'll start a new fleet, a new admiralty, if you let him. So what's it going to be? Your profile says you're high on loyalty. I suppose that means to the fleet or whoever commands it."

Vernier could see up and down the block, but there was nothing yet, no spacecraft, no alien gunslingers, no natives dressed like cavalrymen. He looked back at the woman at the bar, the lovely and dangerous woman he thought he knew so well. "How well do any of us know ourselves?" was the thought that came to mind.

LeGuin heard him through her trans-mentor. "Maybe not as well as others know us."

"And what was that crack about starting a new admiralty? What's wrong with the old one?" He had to ask, even though he thought he knew.

"Gone. Wiped out. The two ships at this planet are all that remains. This badge on my shirt is all that remains of the admiralty."

Vernier shuddered. "What about our crew? Our ship?"

LeGuin got up and came to him, like a mother to a child. "Stay here with me. Let Wells go off and do the impossible. He'll be dead before he sees our world come back to life. I doubt he will make it a year before his ship is found and destroyed."

"What would we do?" Vernier was trying to imagine it.

LeGuin took him in her arms. "Just the two of us?" She looked at him as if searching for stars that had been seen before, as if all she needed was one familiar glimmer. "Our last two crew members died this morning. The ship was burning. I set it for a decaying orbit and came down to find you. We have this one cocoon left, and the one you came in."

Vernier broke away from her. "You could have told me."

LeGuin said, "One of the other things that shows on your profile is a tendency toward hero worship. I was afraid you might latch onto an experienced senior officer. From the sound of that cocoon, Wells doesn't trust you much either. He has come to make sure you do his bidding."

"What is your bidding, commander?" Vernier was playing for time.

"Our mission has changed," said the woman who reached out to him again. "We can't go back. We should stay and keep the memory alive. Someday, we may find others. I can't go looking for them now, not without a ship or crew."

Vernier shook his head. "What about the native crew? We could take them."

"It's not their fight," she said, her eyes glistening. "You said yourself that they are looking for a new home. What happens when they find it? They would be taking us along with them, not the other way around. We might as well stay here and fit in the best we can. We don't need another world, because we've already got one. Let them go."

Vernier stared her down. "What of Wells? He thinks I'm leaving with him."

The woman came and he let her tighten her arms around him. "I don't want you to go," she said in a whisper.

"The other ship needs me" said Vernier. "Maybe you just want someone to tell you that you didn't fail, that it was okay to ditch the ship and bury the dead as a cloud of cinders. Or maybe you're not asking me to do anything, but just keep you company."

"Is that not enough for you?"

Some rustling of windblown weeds was heard on the plank sidewalk outside. Some hanging glass in other windows was making music, like the tinkling of an old piano. "Sentimentality," said Vernier, pushing away, "is not part of my profile."

Then a strong wind raked the windows, accompanied by the whining of a blaster. Vernier poked his head out one of the windows and saw the figure of a single man coming toward them, dressed in the uniform of a troop colonel, advancing steadily.

"Don't go out there," said Vernier when he saw LeGuin lean into the doorway. "I haven't decided anything yet."

LeGuin looked back at him. "That's okay. I can do all the deciding for you. That's what commanders get paid for." Then she sent a low-power beam in his direction and stunned him just as he leaped toward her. He fell at her feet, and she stepped over him and into the brighter light that waited outside.

From his position on the floor, Vernier listened helplessly to everything that happened on the street. Mostly he heard blaster weapons roar and soon there was the scent of burning wood on the earthy wind. He thought he might move an arm or a leg in a few minutes, but by then the fighting would be over.

In fact, it was only another minute before the last shot echoed off the scorched walls and the last glass fell into the dirt. Vernier struggled up, but his whole body ached as if LeGuin had thrown him the way she had that first day of training. He struggled to the doorway and took in the damage. In the middle of the smoldering barber shop porch lay the body of Colonel Wells. One arm was still moving. Closer to the saloon, the body of Light Commander LeGuin was draped over a hitching rail, her head knocking in a nervous twitch against a watering trough.

Vernier clumped across the street to where the colonel lay with a burn mark on his chest. The older officer opened his eyes when he heard footfalls near him. "Oh, glad it's you," he said thickly. "Just time for one thing. Get the books if you can, from my library."

"Shouldn't they stay with the ship?" Vernier wondered out loud.

"Ship's leaving. I told them to launch tonight. Don't know where. Just going before anyone else finds them. Save some, will you? Do it for an old trooper."

"I'll remember."

"Thanks," said Wells, just before his eyes froze and his head turned toward the wall. Vernier felt some stun particles still stinging his bones, but he made it over to the hitching rail by lurching the last few steps. He grabbed LeGuin by the hair and lifted her, not expecting her to respond. She surprised him by opening one eye and smiling from one side of her face. The other side seemed frozen. "Hey, Jay, that you?"

"So we're on a first-name basis now?" said Vernier. He played with the zipper around her neck and tugged at it. The skin underneath was mottled with the advance of radiation sickness. He bit his lip and felt the pain. "You've been keeping the truth from me in more than one way."

"A good life is full of surprises," she said. "Tell me, quickly now. Did you ever decide whose side you were on?" Her voice was as weak as it could be and still be heard.

Vernier bent down and kissed her hard, so that even a half-conscious person might feel it, and believe in it. He couldn't hold it long, because his legs were folding, so he tried to pull her up with him, but wound up falling down next to her. He heard her speak again, before he fainted himself.

Her voice came to him as in a dream. "Yeah, that's a good boy."

THE BLOOD OF FAMILY

by Joriah Wood

M was washing the last heavy, cast-iron pot when she heard a persistent knock at the front door of the orphanage. The sun went down hours ago, and she was just getting ready to prepare for bed. She dried her hands and walked briskly to the door before the late guest might wake one of the children.

Pastor O'Reilly was white as a ghost. His hands shook, and M caught sight of a hastily pocketed flask as the large front door of the orphanage swung open. Before she could greet him, he excitedly poured out his whole story. He talked fast, panicked, stumbling over his words—something M hadn't heard him do in any Sunday service. M would sometimes get visions, and with a flash of premonition she knew what had the old Irishman so shaken. Like a mother comforting her child, she patted him on the back and told him to go home and sleep, reassuring him that she'd take care of things.

M watched him stagger down the dark street by the dim light of the candle-lit lanterns lining the road. He would go home, but she knew he wouldn't be able to sleep. After throwing her warmest shawl over her shoulders, M locked the door and set out for the Jansons' farmhouse.

The cold night air gave her goosebumps, or at least she blamed the night. She wanted to blame the night. She didn't want to acknowledge her own growing fear as she thought about the pastor's words and her vision.

The premonition haunted her as she walked. Every time she closed her eyes, she saw them—yellow eyes, staring at her from the darkness. She smelled the beast's sulfurous breath when she breathed in. The fresh outdoor air masked the stench, but the subtlety of evil remained, needling at her subconscious. The whispering wind, normally comforting, only seemed to mask the hiss of the monster's breath. She felt like she was being stalked, like this thing was behind her, for the entirety of the trip.

At last, M spied the large farmhouse in the distance. She shuddered as she approached. This type of house call was never easy, even though she had more experience with it than she liked to admit.

M scaled the wooden steps quickly and knocked on the door, a quick staccato pattern. As much as she dreaded what she would find inside, she also didn't much enjoy standing in the cold.

The door creaked open and she found herself looking down at the wrinkled and weathered face of a woman, about fifteen years her senior. Mrs. Janson was a farmer, a tough woman who worked the land with her husband and had been doing so since before M drifted into this town.

"Mrs. Janson, Reverend O'Reilly asked me to come by. He said that your daughter was ill, and he thought I might be able to help." M spent much of her time shut up inside the orphanage where she worked, and it occurred to her that she hadn't seen Mr. Janson about town in some months. Life in the western expansion was tough, and she wanted to be sensitive, just in case...

"Please, come in. O'Reilly said to expect you." Mrs. Janson nodded and opened the door wider, motioning M through the gateway into the home. Her face was weary, her eyes hollow, like she hadn't slept in weeks.

She led M down a short hallway, passing a door on either side of them before they arrived at a warm sitting room. A fire blazed in the fireplace, and M was thankful for the heat.

"Sit down, please," Mrs. Janson said. "Can I get you some

tea?"

M shook her head.

"No, thank you, Mrs. Janson," she responded. The air in this room was warm and thick, and M could almost feel a palpable darkness emanating from the back of the large house. She did her best to keep from looking toward it, afraid that Mrs. Janson would be further spooked if she realized that M could sense it. "Please, can you tell me a bit about your daughter?"

Mrs. Janson's back stiffened and her gaze averted, looking past M to the fire.

"I think I'll fix myself some tea, first," she said, her voice wooden.

M nodded.

"Take your time," she said, her voice as soothing as she could manage while her mind screamed for the older woman to hurry.

She must not add to the panic in the house, the fear.

M spied a small shelf of books across the room. While the older woman's back was turned and she prepared her tea, M walked over to examine the texts. She ran her fingers along the spines of the old books, noting works by Benjamin Franklin, Webster's *A Grammatical Institute of the English Language*, and…she paused.

As her index finger traced across a small bundle of loose leaf pages, another vision exploded in her mind. She was ripped from the room, transported instead to a camp in the woods, sometime during the middle of the night. In the time between seconds, a chill grasped her spine that wouldn't let go—she recognized this place.

A large fire burned around her, heating her skin but not burning her, her body protected by the arcane magic conjured by the five men surrounding her. The lines of a pentagram crisscrossed between them, each man standing on a point as the pale one, the leader—Eli—led them in a chant read from an ancient book, written in an old and barely-translatable demonic language. The *Book of Oram*. Eli's face was distorted through the heatwaves of the fire, but the text in front of him glowed with the power of the spoken words.

M knew those words; they were etched in her mind forever, the sound and the power they evoked.

With a start, she was back in the old farmhouse. She jerked her hand away from the papers, her eyes wide, and she glanced at the old woman—still pouring her tea, barely a moment had passed. The unknown fear that gripped her before now had a name, and M didn't have a moment to spare.

"Mrs. Janson, is Mr. Janson…" M let the words fade and linger when she watched the woman's shoulders go rigid.

"He passed away a few weeks ago."

"Oh, I'm sorry to hear of your loss," M quickly responded. M wondered if that could be contributing to the oppressive aura she sensed in the house. "And your little girl?"

Mrs. Janson turned and walked slowly to a large chair near the fire. M could hear the cup rattle against the saucer before Mrs. Janson slowly raised it to her lips.

"Rae Ann took it quite hard, as you might imagine. She was the apple of his eye." She took a sip of tea then lowered the cup slightly, her dark eyes peering at M through the steam. "Not a day went by when he wasn't looking to her future."

M nodded toward the bookshelf. "So, the texts then, she's well educated?"

Mrs. Janson nodded and grunted an approval. "Of course, he insisted on the highest in academics from her. He didn't want her to have to learn to tend a farm, like us." M detected a hint of bitterness in the older woman's voice, but she said nothing.

"And Rae Ann is here, then?"

As if being pulled from a bad memory into a more terrifying future, Mrs. Janson's face lost its color.

"She is here, in the back room. Sleeping right now, I suppose, after…" An uncomfortable look crossed the woman's face as she glanced around—down at her tea cup, the floor beyond it, the wall behind M—anywhere but into M's eyes. "…well, after

O'Reilly left, she was very tired and thought she should rest. And she needs it, she hasn't slept this quietly in a few nights now."

"That's probably for the best," M acknowledged, a picture beginning to form in her mind. "Mrs. Janson, can I ask where your husband is buried?"

"He's out back, underneath the Sycamore tree down a little ways near the pond. He loved that tree. Why?" Her last question caught M a little off guard—it was a challenge.

"I'd just like to see the plot, that's all."

"That would be fine," she said. Mrs. Janson stood and walked over to light a lantern hanging near the door. "O'Reilly said you were an odd stick, but he assured me that you could help. And when a circuit preacher like O'Reilly can't handle something like this…"

"Something like what?" M interjected. It almost seemed like Mrs. Janson was ready to open up about what was going on with her daughter, but the older woman's lips pursed tight.

"Nothing, dear." She offered M the lantern and reiterated her instructions on how to get down to Mr. Janson's grave.

Opening the door, M saw that it was raining. "Are you sure you must go down there?" Mrs. Janson asked, and M nodded.

"I do."

"Then for my daughter's sake," she started, "I sincerely hope you find what you're looking for."

With the lantern held up to light her way, M slogged down a crude trail to the spot where Mr. Janson was buried. The steady rain was turning much of the worn path to mud, and M had to catch her balance as her heeled-boot slipped into a deep divot. It was a footprint, one of many, and it was deep. M stepped carefully, hoping to avoid a twisted ankle, but she was having trouble seeing the mud-slick divots with only the lamp to light her way.

The journey was slow but M eventually found herself down at the sycamore. She had to duck underneath the low branches, but at least the limbs provided some shelter from the rain. She spotted a simple gravestone under the tree, and M held the lantern close enough to read the name on it.

Ezekiel Janson.

Her eyes scanned the writing and numbers below, but it was when M's gaze fell to the dirt that the blood ran cold in her veins.

The soil was overturned, thrown everywhere. Whoever had been buried here was no longer in the ground. Did someone dig up Ezekiel Janson—or did Ezekiel Janson let himself out?

"Life, life…where's the channel to the life?" M muttered under her breath, reconciling what she'd just discovered with her knowledge of occult practices and rituals. She knew how the world worked—how it really worked, anyway, behind the veil of what most people thought of as normality.

She swung the lantern over to the sycamore to examine it. She didn't even have to look closely to see where the bark had been scraped away, leaving a large bare spot of wood, about three feet up from the ground. On the bare spot was carved an arcane symbol that M had seen before. It was a symbol of power, evil power. She fought back panic as her suspicions were confirmed.

The footprints weren't headed to the sycamore from the house— they were headed up to the house from the evacuated grave.

The lantern swung wildly as M took off in a sprint back to the house. Her foot slipped into one of Ezekiel's deep footprints, and she stumbled, falling to the muddy ground but managing to keep the lantern in-hand. She struggled to her feet, a sharp pain shooting from her ankle up through her right leg. She wanted to stop and favor that ankle, but she conjured the image of Mrs. Janson and her daughter, alone in the house with a monster.

She must push forward. M closed her eyes for a moment and imagined herself standing in the void of her mind. Before her was a door, and beyond that door was the pain, trying to get inside. With a grunt, she planted her shoulder into the door and refused to give, no matter how hard the pain would push in.

When she opened her eyes, she was already up and moving toward the house again. Keeping her shoulder firmly on that door in her mind and her teeth clenched, she pressed on. After what felt like an eternity, M reached the front door.

She rapped on the wooden door, hard. "Mrs. Janson!" she called. She tried again, but since time was of the essence she tried the latch, and the door swung open easily. M stepped inside.

"Mrs. Janson!" she yelled, and the older woman appeared from one of the front bedrooms, surprised that M had let herself in.

"My dear, what are you so worked up about?" she asked, perplexed as she looked at M's wet and muddy form.

M reached out and put a hand on Mrs. Janson's shoulder. "Have you checked on Rae Ann recently?" M implored, but Mrs. Janson shook her head.

"No, I haven't…I mean…" she started, stumbling over her answer. "She's been sleeping quietly, I didn't want to disturb her."

M looked at the back of the house. "She's in danger," she said, glancing over to catch the incredulous look from Mrs. Janson.

"O'Reilly said that your ways were…different, but I don't think waking her would be a good idea right now." M ignored the firm look on Mrs. Janson's face and pushed past her, heading for the back room, reaching under her shawl as she did.

Mrs. Janson gave chase, getting a handful of M's jacket and turning the younger woman around. "Just what do you think you're…"

Mrs. Janson stopped talking as she spotted the Colt Single Action Army clasped close to M's chest. Her jaw hung slack as she searched for words.

"Look into my eyes," M implored Mrs. Janson, as she watched the anger of a protective mother creeping across the older woman's face.

Mrs. Janson complied. She watched as a storm of orange and red overtook the iris, rolling like fire over M's naturally hazel color. M watched the woman's face relax as her anger abated.

"Save her," Mrs. Janson said quietly, and she let go. M nodded solemnly, trying and failing to suppress the shudder that ran down her spine. Every time she dipped into the spirit's power, the sensation got stronger. She could tell she would have to let this spirit go soon.

"I just hope it's not too late," M answered.

She turned the knob and threw the door open.

As light from the sitting room spilled into the back bedroom, M saw the silhouette of a young girl, sitting up in bed. Her back was to the door.

"Lantern?" she called over her shoulder, and Mrs. Janson appeared moments later with a lantern. Before M could raise the lamp, lightning flashed and she saw another dark silhouette. The image disappeared quickly, but it burned itself into M's mind.

Mr. Janson was seated in the chair across from the young girl's bed. Slumped over, his hairless head down, his arms fallen by his side, his stomach so bloated it looked like it could burst at any moment.

From behind her, M heard Mrs. Janson gasp. M raised the lantern with her left hand and steeled herself. She'd faced worse than a risen dead before. She wasn't afraid; fear was what you felt before the danger arrived. Now, she only felt purpose.

She took three steps into the room, until she stood just in front of the girl, and M raised the big Single Action Army to draw a bead on Mr. Janson's head.

"You should have stayed in the ground," she said with ice in her voice. The room lit with the muzzle flash as M fired, thumbed the hammer back quickly and fired again.

When her eyes adjusted to the dim light cast from the lantern, M saw Mr. Janson's corpse lying on the ground. The right side of his head was vaporized by the two .45 caliber rounds. His stomach split in the fall from the chair, spilling liquefied insides across the wooden floor. M looked at him curiously; usually, the recently-undeceased twitched a bit immediately post-death.

She stepped closer to peer at the corpse.

She realized that it was, indeed, just a corpse.

M could almost feel the icy breath of the grave on the back of her neck as a low cackle rolled through the room. "How long have you had her?" M asked.

"Long enough to grant her wish and fulfill my end of the bargain," the voice floated to her ears from the bed, the sweet voice of a fifteen-year-old girl twisted with the wrought-iron bars of Hell and mixed with the black inferno itself. "She wanted her daddy out of the ground, and was willing to trade nearly anything for it."

M slowly turned, keeping the Army revolver close to her chest again, swinging the lantern around to look at the girl. She stared into wild, yellow eyes—the eyes of the possessed. The girl's white nightgown clung to her body, wet and slick with the outdoor mud.

"So you helped her dig up the corpse and bring it here," M said. "You tricked her."

The girl's face twisted into a wicked grin, her lips stretching abnormally far from her teeth, exposing them to the root. "I did. And now, her body is mine. You know the rules."

M knew them well. The papers she touched contained passages from the *Book of Oram*, a text that specialized in the calling of demons. She had heard those words at the ritual she barely escaped from, years ago; the one that changed her into who she was today, an unhinged soul that could be easily possessed if she left the door unguarded.

Five brothers, having already been trading parts of their souls to the demons in exchange for power, had captured her and intended to make her an unwilling member of their unholy cadre. They managed to open a door into her soul with words from the book, but she fought back. She kept the demon trying to possess her at bay much in the same way that she kept the pain away earlier, by closing the door to it with sheer willpower. To her good fortune, a benevolent spirit—the spirit of a great wolf— heard her cries for aid and helped her fight the demon away. She greeted the wolf spirit as a guest, and the spirit then assisted her in escaping from the brothers.

Unfortunately for M's sanity, she couldn't lock that door anymore. She learned many things: that spirits could easily find and possess her, if she wasn't wary; that there were both evil and good spirits; and that spirits could only reside in her for so long before they would have to move on. Fortunately, she'd managed to keep the demons at bay thus far, but her increased sensitivity to them made every confrontation with one dangerous to her mind.

"Leave her now," M stated, thumbing the hammer back on the revolver.

"Why should I?" the demon cackled. "You're going to shoot a young girl? You, the woman who spends her time working with orphans and helping children?"

M's breath caught in her throat. How did the demon know her so well?

As if it could read her thoughts, the girl's mouth moved once more. "Oh, you're well-known, you and that pesky friend of yours. We know all about both of you."

M knew the demon was talking about Devil, a man she'd traveled and fought with before, someone who had also put down his share of the possessed.

But the demon's words caused M to hesitate, and that's all it wanted.

The sound of tearing muscle and ripping sinew heralded the bursting of bloody, leathery bat-like wings from the young girl's back. Before M's eyes, the girl transformed, her eyes bulging out of their sockets, her tongue lolling out beyond her slack jaw and falling nearly to her chest. Long black claws sprouted from the girl's fingers.

M fired three times, thumbing the hammer as fast as she could as she backed deeper into the room. She couldn't see through the thick cloud of gunsmoke, but she was close enough that the slugs must have all struck home.

When the smoke cleared, she saw the beast standing in front of her, and too late she realized that her shots had been low—the demon had leapt to its feet as the first shot was fired. Blood ran down its legs where the slugs had torn through them, but it still stood.

Black ichor dripped down from the beast's long tongue to the sweat-stained nightgown, and its claws clacked against each other as it stared hungrily at M. Unconsciously, she shrank away from it, realizing that she was out of ammunition—she always left one chamber empty to carry the pistol safely.

The beast met her eyes, and she saw the distinct look of the hunter evaluating its prey. With a triumphant howl and a swoosh of its leathery wings, it leapt at her.

M closed her eyes and looked at the door in her mind again, the speed of thought slowing time around her. This wasn't like the pain she shut out, earlier—this was a much more vivid vision, one that was always tucked into the corner of her consciousness.

She stood staring at the door opened by the brothers that night during the ritual. The door was closed now, but unlike then, she knew which spirit stood beyond it.

Her hand trembled as she touched the latch. She took a deep breath and threw it open.

Standing on the other side was an old man, the lines in his face deep, having seen many sunrises and sunsets. He stood on the other side of the door, patient, waiting for her, the wolves at his feet sitting just as composed.

"Come in," M said to him, and he smiled and nodded knowingly. She knew that this would be the last time she could let him in—every spirit could only tarry for so long—and when he left, she would once again have to guard the door vigilantly.

But she needed the wolven spirit now.

When her eyes blinked open, the monstrous demon was nearly through the air and on top of her. She met its hungry gaze with ferocity, her iris and pupil now black but crisscrossed by the five flaming lines of the pentagram reflected from the ritual so long ago. The demon winced as it realized what was happening, but it was too late. Her transformation was already in effect.

By the time it landed on her, M was possessed completely

by the wolven spirit. The demon descended claw-first, but her supernaturally-lithe body twisted beneath it as blood and gray fur fell to the floor. With a snarl, the demon flew off of her body, and she snapped to her feet.

Her visage darkened, M's mouth hung open, the still-vaguely human shape of it barely able to contain the rows of sharpened teeth. Short, sharp claws protruded from her fingertips. Her dress was torn where the demon's claws made contact, blood matting the fabric, nearly doubling her over in pain, but even hunched over, she raised her head to the demon. She was wounded, but she wasn't prey.

The demon righted itself and stood to consider her, sizing up her new form. There was almost no recollection of Rae Ann's form anymore as it stood full-upright, towering over M. Her claws had found their mark though, leaving long gashes from the demon's neck to its belly, spilling more of the demon's black blood on the floor of the farmhouse.

It was wounded, but clearly less so than M, and both combatants realized this at the same time. The demon lunged again. M tried to defend herself, scratching and snapping her jaws as it pinned her, but it rolled her back to the floor and held her there. The demon's long tongue hung from its mouth and M's canine-like jaws snapped at it, but the snake-like appendage managed to slither and twist just out of her reach. Sensing impending victory, the monster was toying with her.

The blast of the shotgun inside the confines of the house was deafening, especially to M's more sensitive hearing in the wolven form. Her eyes shut tight as the pain arced between her ears, but she was aware of the sensation of warm drops of blood spraying across her face and the shifting weight of the demon. Instead of controlling her, holding her down, it slumped against her, becoming dead weight. The shotgun roared again, and M couldn't help but yip in pain at the sound again. She let the pain fuel her as she twisted the demonic form off of her, rolling away from it.

In the doorway stood Mrs. Janson, the smoking barrels of the double-barreled shotgun against her shoulder telling the entire story. The demon looked at the older woman, surprise in its eyes as it tried to hold its intestines in with its clawed hands. The holes left by the shotgun were too large, and it couldn't stop the cascade of black blood.

The ripped and tattered nightgown, the last remnant of Rae Ann, lay on the floor nearby.

M forced herself to stand, towering over the dying demon. She grabbed its hair with one hand and with three heavy swipes from the other, she managed to sever the thing's head, tossing it dismissively to the floor next to the body.

Then she closed her eyes.

In her mind, she smiled at the old man as he and his wolves departed. She wanted to thank him, but she didn't have to. He knew, smiling at her and giving a small wave as he departed through the door. As she closed it behind him, she wondered which spirit would knock at the door next.

And she continued to watch the door in her dreams, as her body slipped into unconsciousness.

M woke up disconcerted. She panicked, sitting up quickly, but Mrs. Janson put a reassuring hand on her shoulder.

"You're in my bed," she offered, and the memories came flooding back. M collapsed back into the pillow, her side and her ankle both aching something fierce. She turned to look at Mrs. Janson, whose eyes were red and swollen from crying. She had moved M to the bed and tended to her wounds, probably preferring to keep busy in hopes that it would take her mind off of the night's events.

M knew the feeling only too well.

"I wish I could say it would all be ok…" M started, but Mrs. Janson only nodded as she screwed her face up, trying not to cry in front of the younger woman. "Where is the body?"

Mrs. Janson gestured toward the back of the house. "Lying

where it fell in the back room. I've bolted the door," she said, her face easing as she recounted the facts like a teacher might recite times-tables to their class.

M relaxed her head back into the pillow. "We'll have to burn the house," she said, her heart aching for the woman, but Mrs. Janson just nodded.

"I thought we might," she said. "Fitting end, I guess. They'll both be buried in the house we all built together." Emotion overcame her as the words tumbled out, and Mrs. Janson was crying again. M looked away, wanting to give the woman whatever privacy she could.

After a moment, M reached a hand out, which Mrs. Janson took into her own.

"There are some papers I need to retrieve from your shelf before we leave," M said. "But then, we really should get going. You're welcome to come with me, back to the orphanage." Mrs. Janson looked like she was about to cry again, at the thought of being around children, but M continued quickly. "You'd be my guest, of course. Take time to heal, and you can decide what to do from there." Mrs. Janson nodded quickly.

"Let me pack my things."

Smoke billowed from the windows of the farmhouse as the flames took hold of it. Mrs. Janson, holding a bag of her belongings over one shoulder and supporting M with her other arm, turned to watch fingers of fire lick the outside of the windows.

"Everything we worked so hard to build," she said, her words weighted with undeniable sorrow. M nodded and squeezed Mrs. Janson's shoulder.

"They'll be waiting for you in the ever-after," she said quietly as Mrs. Janson turned away from the burning farmhouse, her eyes welled with tears once more.

M clutched the satchel with the pages from the *Book of Oram* in it. She didn't dare touch them again, especially right now, but she couldn't run the risk of anyone else finding them either.

She'd already seen these pages destroy too many lives, and she wouldn't let that happen again.

THE CONSERVATOR

by Cecelia Chapman

"...yes, yes, we just got here." The conservator was on the phone with the front office. "I want a new scout. And a new contract. We came for the eclipse, but there's a storm. Zero visibility. I asked the V6 conservator to transfer us...yes, the scout set up perimeter systems..........I think.........they.....cut me off..."

"...so what, Von's on his way." The partner was indifferent.

"This is a volatile situation you are attempting to resolve." They both knew I was lying.

I was going to lose points for that call. So what? The front office only wants to know the contract is complete. And everyone knew the conservator and her partner were hostile customers. If I didn't need money for a project I wouldn't be on this job. And it was over tomorrow.

Securing the conservator's rancho and villa took ten days. Cameras and lasers were sited. Metal, motion and heat detectors studded trees and rocks. An intercept dome lined the perimeter of the rancho to the canyon edge where guerrillas lived in the walls. The landing craft was safe in the underground stall. Should I sleep in it tonight near the conservator and her partner? They were going to be pissed when their friend, Von, couldn't land.

The conservator and her partner were still arguing so I looked through their well-documented art collection.

Betelgeus death traps, Sythian blades, Xenoj glasses, Jguq

claws, Ter jaws, Mars mummies, crumbled Tyryx sculpture. The artifacts were waiting for the curator. Live streaming bondo art club holograms glittered between broken mosaics depicting humans being ripped apart by animals. Gliese 581-d ikons lay in a broken pod. The time portal kept morphing. It annoyed me. File pods, screens, veo veils, outerworld fetishes, old world paintings lay in stacks everywhere. Rare malignant, mobile black-holes clustered in corners, around sculpture. Art auction numbers flashed on the curator's desk.

I wondered about my projects. Would they end up like this? In a jumbled pile where no one could possibly experience them.

After a while the conservator and her partner calmed down and I returned to my camp outside.

Wind-swept clouds raced across the purple sunset, turning it black. The curved rancho villa walls slithered in the flickering light. Rising from underground living space to the conservator's gallery above ground, the villa then slid back into the earth where it housed the vehicle stall.

Blinking aerial habitats filled the night skies. It seemed like the entire Earth population was overhead in their Council-mandated orbit, jockeying for position to watch the eclipse. I watched Von's conservators' vehicle hovering in the crowd. Marked with Environmental and Cultural Guardian insignia, the designated crafts were symbol of the conservator's exclusive status to live on-planet. Von tried to land again and flew off.

I noticed some of the tiny white fish smoking in the fire were gone. Just as I decided it was probably the small masked animal watching me for days, a woman walked out of the canyon. She lifted her arm to push her hair under her hat, the fringe on her jacket whipped out like wings in the wind. In the seconds the moon emerged from the clouds, I saw she wore a bandolier filled with ammunition. I did not see a weapon.

"How did you break my perimeter?"

"You feel safe sleeping outside?"

"It's against my contract to harm unarmed beings."

"Not mine." She took a blackened fish from the flames and tossed it in her mouth. Then she picked another.

"What do you want?"

…a terrible, scratching, screech sound stopped us. The villa's stall door was being opened manually. We could hear the conservator and her partner arguing.

"Don't move, they might harm you." The woman's hand slapped down hard on my thigh.

"Can they start the craft without you?"

"Yes."

"Can they operate it?"

"…if they can figure out automatic…but they can't fly it without me."

A crowd appeared, climbing out of the canyon, rolling boulders to block the stall. Kidnap. I sighed.

"We don't want the conservator."

"What do you want?"

"We want the conservator and friend out of here. You can take them back."

"…I'll lose my license, the contract…"

She made a laughing, snorting sound at that and stood up. When she bent over me I recognized her at once.

"You have choices…"

Finding her there was incredible. The thought of capturing her, returning to claim a huge bounty…

"How long do you have in this…occupation?" She took another fish and waved it at me. "We'll leave you alone. But go. Now!"

I was shaking. I can't remember walking to the villa. The conservator's face was green in the craft's panel lights. When I jumped inside the vehicle the crowd started rolling the rocks away.

"You…" The partner pointed a finger at me.

"I don't want to hear anything from you two. You were going to steal my craft. If you didn't open the stall door you would be safe inside. They are letting us go but your villa will be looted and trashed and I'll lose my license."

I pushed the conservator and friend hard, back into the cargo area of the vehicle.

"Get in there, I don't even want to see you. When we get to the transfer port I'll file a report with the authorities." Suddenly I decided to lock the cargo door.

Sweat poured through my clothes. My hands fumbled the control panel setting coordinates for automatic pilot. I knew I was making a rash decision but my body was no longer mine. I jumped to ground and the craft lifted into the night without me.

ABOVE SNAKES

by John Medaille

Part 1 - The Guy with the See-Through Skin

A three days' ride through lava desert thick with Martian lions and cyclones brung Choppy and me to the meeting place, and by the end of it I was considerable nettled. It weren't that I begrudged Choppy as a pardner, it's jest the sloshing sound he made when he moved. Choppy wore him an old space suit, and by old I mean old-old, like the kind all them old cosmonauts and astronauts useta wear backaways in the beginning of things, 'ceptin' he'd kitted his out with gunbelts and an armpit holster and the chaps and spurs and, acourse, the sombrero. He never took it off, not that I ever seen, not so much as the boots. It's from inside his digs that that sloshin' sound came, and I was never for certain if the sloshin' come from a bath that Choppy carries around with himself in there or if the bath *was* Choppy, and if it's the suit that's all what held him together. More than once I been tempted to perforate him jest to find out which, specially after a three days hard ride listening to the slosh. Jest plug him quick and see what comes runnin' out the holes. I mighta done it if it weren't that Choppy weren't three times as quick on the draw as a pistolero as what I am. Which he is.

The meetin' place was a little saloon called The Lady Chance in Ogallala. We reined up in the arcade and bowlegged it across the planks, our heels raisin' the thin, red dust that covers the county. It's jest like all these nothin' prairie towns, an unglorious place to go and get ourselves kilt.

It was dark inside The Lady Chance, but I seen a piebald faro table, a shelf full of red liquor, a few cowpunchers drinkin' it and a couple of surly goodnight girls, them and at a table by his lonesome I saw our guy, the guy with the see-through skin.

We sidled up to him and I said, "You the guy?"

And he said, "Yes, I'm the guy, Mr. Lowell."

"That's right, I'm Lowell." I cocked a thumb back at Choppy. "And this here's Schiaparelli."

Choppy don't say nothin', cause Choppy never does. But there's a deep sea gurgle inside his suit, cheap coffee percolatin'.

"I am John Membraneous," said the guy, "the Eight-Thousandth and Fifty-Sixth Clansman of the House of Barboa. Have a seat."

I scraped up a chair and ordered mescal. The barman brung it, all the time giving our guy The Eye. Choppy remained in the upright.

The guy's was an Easterner and looked like the weak sister. Got on an accountant's suit, and he had him a cravat with a uranium stickpin in it. Inside the guy I saw his organs floatin' and bobbin', his small teeth and the pink eel that's his tongue. The stalks of his eyes swirled and disappeared down the stiff collar of his boiled shirt. His brain must have been down there somewheres. I seen something I don't know what thumpin' up near the inside of his scalp, thing like a big kidney bean with ganglions coming out of it.

"Why're we here, Membraneous?" I says.

"Why *are* you here, Mr. Lowell?" he said back.

"We heard there was work."

"There is. Tell me, Mr. Lowell, have you ever heard of *The Sic Semper?*"

I thought this out. "Suppose I have."

"And what have you heard?" the guy said. He took a drink and in the gaslight that run through him I seen the alcohol blending with his own jelly, makin' a ripple like heat haze on hardpan.

"Seems I've heard harpooners tell of it. It's a spook story, ain't it? They say it's a ship they see out there, out in the Old Earth/ Mars corridor. A white ship they see out the portholes, but it don't show up on the scopes, do it? And it don't respond to hails and it don't raise no colors. And they look back and it's gone. A ghost ship."

"Yes indeed, Mr. Lowell. A Flying Dutchman."

"You say so. Some of these sailors say it's crewed by skeletons and Satans and what-the-hell all else. I've heard a parcel of simlar stories off old sailors, Membraneous. All the used-up ones ain't got nought else to do but smoke themselves to death and tell raw ones 'bout all the haints and spook-lights they seen. I've heard tell of asteroids filled with naked wimmin' and space monsters down in the deeps. But I ain't never saw fit to hold no truck with them. So I'll ask you agin', why're we here?"

Membraneous said, "I am here because I am a prospector and speculator, Misters Lowell and Schiaparelli. I make and lose fortunes, that is what I do. I've made and lost several on the Martian frontier already. You are here because I sent for you, because I am in need of men with your particular proclivities in my current venture. I am in need of killers. Of desperadoes and cruel men. You, Mr. Lowell, are a gunslinger of no small skill. You were in Moxley's Rough Riders and fought on Phobos and Eros. Presently, you are a wanted man in Mexador and Exoduster. Is that not so?"

"I reckon it is."

"And your partner, Mr. Schiaparelli, is better known as the bandito Stagolee, and who is wanted from Jupiter to Venus. Who, if I'm not mistaken, was marooned on Mercury by The Wonderful Brain, and who is currently thought to be dead. Is that not so?"

"I couldn't say."

"But he was, at one time, a prisoner of Mercury?"

"I couldn't rightly say where he's been or hasn't."

"Fair enough. We are here because there is killing to be done and money to be gotten from the doing of it."

I drank my drink. "And it's got to do with *The Sic Semper*."

"It does indeed. You are quite right concerning the legends of the ghost ship. They are nothing but seamen's opium dreams. There was, however, an actual, historical *Sic Semper*. It was one of the first refugee ships to leave Old Earth after the Apocalypse. There were five thousand souls on board headed to Mars to start an American colony. It never arrived. It was last seen beyond Star of India Station, and then promptly disappeared. Its wreck was never found. That is the basis for the fables you have heard. Further, there is this; all of the passengers on board *The Sic Semper* were exceedingly wealthy. In those first days, only the very rich could afford passage off Earth. On the ship were three of the ten richest living humans at that time. There was royalty: queens, princes, sheiks, caliphs, emperors. Four of the cloned Mad Kings of St. Helena were on board. Officers of Thinking Machines Unlimited were there, and the entire Board of Directors of U.S. Reactor. The AllFaith Pope had purchased passage, as well as an infinity of movie stars, icons, heiresses, moguls, crimelords and geniuses. Old money and new. All aboard a single vessel, lost with all hands."

I ordered another drink, but I never was no good with the drink. No stomach. "So?" I said.

"Just so, Mr. Lowell. So whatever these passengers did not pay out for their fare, they took with them as commodity. None of them ever expected to return to Earth. They took all they had, and not in currency. So much of the wealth of Old Earth was liquidated in a matter of days, into antiquities, art, precious metals and rare elements. *The Last Supper*, The Rosasharn, *American Gothic*, all spirited away, overnight. Lost to history and memory. So much of it has never been found, not to this day. Records from the period are imprecise and no bills of sale were made. It can be safely assumed that a substantial portion of these treasures were secreted away in the cargo hold of *The Sic Semper*. Did you know that three days after The Apocalypse, when Marietta's Ebola had been released and the Easter Crusade was advancing on New York City, the Statue of Liberty just disappeared? Leaving an empty island? What if it were on *The Sic Semper*? The timing is right. Do have any idea of what its value would be today?"

"So?"

"So, as I am sure you have assumed, *The Sic Semper* has been found."

"Yeah?"

"Yes, Mr. Lowell." Something like a spleen drifted up passed the guy's collar, and sorta nosed around behind the guy's eyebrow, then it drifted away. "Yes, quite. South of here in Have Gun, three hundred miles below Fort Ares and the Agua Frio. You're familiar with the area?"

I considered. "Downaways in New South Hell?"

"Precisely."

"Bad country," I said.

Choppy gurgled in back of me.

"Are you familiar with it?"

"I been there, but ain't nobody what you'd call on friendly terms with it. Bad country."

"Yes, Mr. Lowell, that is my understanding. There are magnetic irregularities in the atmosphere."

"Irregularities? Machines don't work there, Membraneous, they flame out and dive. Strange rays come out of the ground to blow the ass end off you. The place is circled with a ring-a-rosie of wrecked hoppers and triplanes. We'd have to ride in on jackrabbits, and when you're on the ground there's nothing but dust devils and arterioforms and cacti. No water, no food, cold as Tartarus. It's a triangle for starving in. Membraneous, that country'll regulate your gaddam account for you."

"Which is why I need men of your quality."

"What makes you so sure your ship is there?"

"I have evidence, Also, the atmospheric irregularities make it the logical place for such a vessel to have floundered and crashed."

"Let's hear yer 'evidence'."

"I purchased what evidence I have from a Martian half-breed named See-No-Evil. Last year he was employed as a mule skinner for a cavalry regiment charged with the extermination of a band of Neo-Apaches who were making raids on Fort Ares and Lincoln. The Apaches were using New South Hell as a refuge and base of operations. The regiment followed them there. See-No-Evil was the only party to escape the fracas, both the Apaches and the cavalry are no more. It took him two months to extricate himself from the region, and by the end of it a substantial portion of his mind was gone, but he found *The Sic Semper*."

"The proof?"

"It is within my keeping. He brought with him daguerrotypes of the wreck, as well as maps, coordinates and a fragment of the hull. I have verified its authenticity to my satisfaction."

"Sounds like the razoo."

"It is all quite valid, Mr. Lowell. I assure you."

"And this See-No-Evil, why didn't he take the treasure himself?"

"He was not aware of the full scope of what he had found. He saw the name of the ship written on the bulkhead, but he failed to make the connection with *The Sic Semper* of legend and lore. At no time did he enter the vessel. He was largely insane at the time, I understand."

"Sane enough to keep some saleable souvenirs."

"Just so. He only realized the potential value of his find much later, when he had been saved by the Mission at Bradbury. By the time I came across him and bought his intelligence, he was selling his secret for whiskey money."

"And what makes you think this half-breed ain't out right now, telling every damfool what comes along about the find?"

A polyp poked its way through the juice of the guy's drinking hand, and it looked at me and did itself a little dance. "Because I murdered him. What concerns me more, Mr. Lowell, is those parties to whom he sold the secret before I disposed of him. I know that there are such parties, but have no positive identification. See-No-Evil was in the throes of *delirium tremens* when I questioned him on such points. But make no mistake, there are such other interested investors who are making their way to New South Hell as we speak. Some of their number have, no doubt, breached its borders already. This is why I have need of gunslingers."

There was a call over a ways from the bar: "Hey, bug!"

Membraneous ignored it. He said, "Time is of the essence, Misters Lowell and Schiaparelli, and I have squandered too much of it already in waiting for your arrival."

"Hey, bug!" the call came again acrost the saloon. "Hey you, maggot!" It was a local rube, a big sodbuster, leaned up against the player piano. He was cyborg, big, black iron pistons and wheels pushed up through the muscles on his arms and in his shoulders. He'd got his load on, too, and his boiler burned hot.

Membraneous don't bat an eyeball, but he's like to play the soft-handed type.

"I said, 'Hey,'" said the character at the pianola. "I'm a-talkin' to you, Venusian." He sauntered over to our table, clomping on pig-metal hooves. "Don't make like you don't hear me. We here's a pure and unmisegenated folk in these parts. Best not let the sun set on you in Ogallala, maggot."

The guy don't turn his eyes from me, but out from behind his chair his coattails flapped up and out come a flagellum. It was as see-through as the rest of him, and full of little yeller sacs and glands and it's got a pricker at the end of it, curved roundabout like a scorpion's stinger. The pricker buried itself into the cyborg's neck, pumped once, then the tail retracted back into the seat of the guy's pants, quick as anything. The cyborg boy stood there for a minute walleyed, not yet knowin' he'd got himself pricked. "Don't let the sun set on you...don't let the sun..." he stammered, and then timbered down backwards, deader'n hell.

"Some trick," I said.

"Here are my terms, Mr. Lowell. You and your associate

will escort me to the wreck of *The Sic Semper*, and of course it is imperative that on the way you shall eliminate any other contenders to the prize. Once we reach the site, we shall make inventory of the find and erect such improvements and beacons in the area so as to secure my legal claim to it in advance of a future mining operation. Mr. Schiaparelli and yourself will act as my bodyguards, my enforcers, my surveyors, and my witnesses. In return for these services you two will share a five percent stake in the future proceeds of the mine, plus any spoils you can carry out from the initial expedition without being found in forfeiture of your primary obligations to me. No monies in advance. These are my terms."

There was nothin' for us, right then, on the horizon. No funds nor backers. It was this, or sure as all hell, me and Choppy would fall to rustlin' and devilment again.

"Okay," I said.

Behind me in The Lady Chance there was that sloshin'. Dried-up waves on a thirsty shore.

Part 2 - New South Hell

We found McLaren's jackrabbit, a red and white pinto, dead on the rim of a crater, and the cactus was eatin' it. Them early terraformers bombarded Mars with mutts, figurin' whatever was fit to live would and whatever wasn't wouldn't, but what Mars sees as fit to live ain't always proper. The cactus was one of the smaller breeds, about five hundred pounds and it dragged itself about on two stubby chicken legs what sprouted out from its undersides. With its thorns it was taking the flesh off McLaren's jackrabbit and absorbin' it. The legs was skelertonized already. The cactus was slow to begin with and occupied at its supper, but Choppy kept his carbine drawn on it all the same. The rabbit had a hole blown in its flank with buckshot from the shootout. We also seen icicles of dark blood frozen and pooled on its saddle and quirt. Happy red drops led away from the cactus and the rabbit, up over the crater's rim, where McLaren musta gone.

I clambered up the ledge with Choppy at my left and John Membraneous bringin' up the rear. I took a look over the rim into the crater and there was a ringin' shot from out the pit and a chunk of Mars not two fingers from my nose was blasted into powder. We three skedaddle down a coupla feet, out of range.

I took the bandanna away from my mouth, and called out over the rim, "Hey, McLaren!"

He called back, "Hey, yerself! That you, Lowell?"

"Yeah!"

"Thought that was you. Choppy there?"

"Yeah, he's here."

"Well, hey to you, Choppy."

Choppy sloshed.

I cried out, "Yer bleedin', McLaren. You been shot?"

There was nothin' from the crater for a bit. Then he said, "Yeah."

"In the guts?"

"Yeah."

A cold wind come up. Behind us, our jackrabbits whickered where we'd tied 'em. They didn't like so much bein' close to the cactus, and they smelled them some rabbit blood on the air. They was spookified.

"Is Steubins dead?" McLaren called.

"Yeah, he's dead."

"How 'bout The Jennifers?"

"They's all dead, too."

"Ain't that a shame. You mean to do me in too, Lowell?"

"Fraid so."

McLaren was silent in the pit for a moment. "How you mean to do it?"

So I told him, "Well, sir, the way I reckon it is we'll flank you all around this here crater, take you from three points and git you in a crossfire. What you think?"

"You might could do. But I got me some good cover down

here, could git a good bead on all a' you. You'd prolly git me in the
end, but I'd git at least one a' you. Might be two."

There was the wind and the neighing of the rabbits and the
click of thorn against bone and the cactus slurpin'. And under all
these there was the everlastin' slosh.

"Or," said McLaren, "you might play it this way, Lowell. You
wait till I bleed out and sleep, then you come on down here
and stretch my neck proper, as nice as you please. Acourse, I'm
gutshot, but beyond that I feel rugged and hale. I figure I'll last at
least eight hours afore I pass out. Maybe more'n. And you'll never
know when I'm playin' possum or not. But even so, it'll be full dark
by the time I'm nibblin' the black loam, and you'll have gone and
lost a full twenty hours on the way to the bonanza. Yer in a hurry,
I reckon. Asides us, and you, did you know Marshall Hazelford
's on his way out here right now? With a bunch a' Comanches he
went and deppetized. He set out from Bradbury not long after
we did. I also heard that half-breed went and sold the coordinates
to Thursday and Durston, too. And them's only the ones I know
about. There's prolly more. Every second you kill here a-killin'
me, that's one second more the further away the prize. They'll
git there first and you'll be suckin' hind tit. Now, let me ask you,
why you want to put yerself all through that botheration and fret,
since I'm gutshot anyways and like to die? Why not saddle up and
ride off into the West. Think of all them riches. All that boodle.
They tell you about all them pretty paintings what's supposed to
be there? What do you say, Lowell?"

I looked back to Membraneous. He'd got him a slouch hat on,
a-coverin' his eyes. He shook his head slow, back and forth and
back again.

"Fraid not," I called out.

"Well, you'll have your way, then," McLaren cries.

I looked down out over New South Hell. Acrost the range, I
seen a herd of cacti loping this way. They'd heard the gunshot and
was hungry. Only the hearty and evil strains survived out here; tall
saguaro with their little arms, prickly pear with their millipede legs

and tiny black eyes, organ pipe a hunnert feet high and flailing.

"Look, McLaren," I called, "here's what it is. Either we do you fast or the cacti come and do you slow. They's on their way."

"I'll take the slow trail."

"Maybe we could come to a deal."

"You ain't got nothin' I want, Lowell."

"Listen here: you throw down yer shootin' irons and we come down and kill you, fast and pleasant and peaceful-like."

"No soap."

I pressed on. "Once we've done it, I save your blood in an opodeldoc jar I got. It'll keep nice and frozen till we get back to Fort Ares, and I'll git you cloned. It won't even cost me a thing cause, I don't know what he was plannin', but Steubins had thirty-five hunnert dollars on him, American money, an I got it right here. That's the deal I'm offerin', McLaren, an I never done yet welshed on a deal."

The crater puzzled this over. "Naw," he said finally. "I jest don't trust you, Lowell."

"There ain't no call for that, to go doubtin' my good word. I'll swear on any grave you say for me to swear on. I ever done you wrong?"

"Not till you bushwhacked me this mornin'."

"Asides that. And ain't it worth the chance? To live and be whole, ruther than in a pit and dead and dry bones without nothin'? Them seems to me to be fair odds."

"Now, Lowell, I do apologize. I don't mean to go doubtin' yer honrable intentions. But all the same...no, I do believe I'll decline. It's jest, it wouldn't be me, you reckon? This clone?"

I told him, "I guess not."

"Well, then," McLaren said.

"Well, then," I said.

We waited for an hour. The cactus clicked at its meal. Choppy done scouted the opposite end of the crater, and there he took a quick poke over the rim, tryin' to git a fix on McLaren, but McLaren was quick as ever and put near blew Choppy's helmet off with his Winchester. Steady hand for a half-dead man. We waited two more hours. There was nothin' left of the jackrabbit but the head and a spit-out burial mound of skinny bones. The great herd of cacti on the horizon kept it's gallivantin' to the crater. They were less'n a mile from us now, and we'd have to git soon, whether the murder was done or not.

There was a low moan from the pit.

I called, "You ailin'?"

McLaren said, "Yessir."

"Gonna get worse."

"I spect so."

The cactus chewed its grub.

McLaren hollered, "Lowell, you still in mind to make a deal?"

"Yeah, I guess."

"All right. You can come on down here and kill me, but you got to give me something in return."

"What's that?"

"A hand."

"What you mean?"

"You got to give me one a yer hands."

A freezing gale blew out of the east, carrying red dust and grit. Comin' up a storm. "What you want that for?"

"Well, I don't want it, not to do nothing with it. But the way I figure it is, there was five of us and three of you. Ya'll killed four, and I'll make an even five, and there's still three of you. I don't think it's fittin' that the three of you should come away without a mark. So one of you fellas got to cut off his hand and throw it in here to me, so I'll have shown you. I ain't askin' you to let me blow off one a' yall's heads, but I don't think that a hand is too much to ask. It ain't right that an enemy should up and kill me, me and The Jennifers, and not have nothin' to show for it. And we's enemies, right?"

I said, "We's enemies." And I looked to Membraneous. "Your show," I whispered to him.

McLaren called, "Well?"

Membraneous don't look at me, but he undoes the glove on his sinister hand, and held it out. Got things floatin' in it, a swarm of little, bitty animicules.

"Okay," I cried out. "We'll fade you, McLaren! Now here's how we'll work this. You toss that Winchester, then I'll toss in the hand to you, then you throw out those pistols I know you got, and then we come in. Agreed?"

"Agreed."

"You ain't got no more guns than that? No derringer or some such?"

"Naw."

"Okay, toss the rifle."

In the pit, we heard the clang of metal against rock. Choppy crept thirty yards to the north, then poked his head up over the rim fast, then down. He nodded at me.

"Where's that there hand?" McLaren called.

"It's comin'," I took my Bowie knife out its scabbard. Membraneous hasn't moved the held-out hand, not a jot. "Right or left, McLaren?"

"Don't keer."

I took the blade and sawed through Membraneous' wrist. I didn't want to touch him. His jelly skin was cold and soft and sickly and the knife went through like it was oleo. He sucked in his breath but he don't pull away. He does not waver nor sway. There weren't no blood. When it's off, John Membraneous cradled the stump, stuck it inside his duster like Napoleon did.

"Here it comes!" I said, and lobbed the hand into the crater. It felt bad against my own hand when I throwed it. The fingers danced and tried to clutch me, reaching out for me in its arc to come and dismember me, a croaker hand. It disappeared into the mouth of the pit and there's a wet thud down there.

"What the hell's that?" McLaren yelled.

"A hand like what you bargained for!"

"It that the foreigner you ridin' with's hand?"

"Yep."

McLaren grumbled from the crater. I don't catch what he said. "How's that?"

"Okay," he called.

"The pistols."

"Yeah. The pistols," he said.

Two hard thunks against the crater walls, one then the other.

"Okay, boys," McLaren yelled. "Getting' on time for my great reward!"

I signaled to Choppy. He unslung his carbine and sited down it over the rim. "Bring the hand," Membraneous whispered to him. Then Choppy climbed over and moved down into the hollow. We didn't hear nothin' from the crater. Ten minutes passed, then he comes on out. He dropped the hand, still twitchful, in the dust before us. Membraneous picked it up and stuck it in his gunbelt.

"There wasn't any gunshot," he said.

"He's dead," I told him.

"You're positive?"

"Go check for yerself, you want."

He said, "Let's go."

We go back to our rabbits and git. As we rode out acrost the badlands, I looked back and seen the herd of cacti. They'd made it to the crater and they crawl and trot and snake their way on in. By the time the dust and the distance obscure them, the crater was a pot of thorns and vegetable matter entwisted and twined about itself, at its feed at the bottom.

I was too far-off to hear, but I already knew what it sounds like.

Part 3 - The Wreck of The Sic Semper

Once I killed me a Martian Catholic priest down in Mexador, but it weren't no sin cause he weren't no good. It was in this little mission out by Matamoros, and after I'd gone and put three balls in his head, I took a gander around his church at all the Holy Santos on the walls. One of them was St. Sebastian, carven out of mesquite. He was a fella tied to a tree of his own and shot through twenty're more times with arrows. Had him a faraway look in his wooden eyes, lookin' skywards, up at God or Mars or whatever else ranges up thataways. He was naked and the arrows done pierced his liver and his arms and his kidneys and his throat and ribs, through one sinew and out the other. He bled red varnish. I looked at the statue a long time that night.

That's what Choppy looked like now, slumped low on his rabbit, his three-hunnert year old gloves loose on the bridle. He was shot through what-all with arrows too, 'ceptin' his arrows were Comanche instead of Roman. Yellow feathers, clumped with gore, fluttered at their tails and flint arrowheads glinted black where they come out of him. Any curiosity I ever kept about what was in his suit was long done satisfied. Thick syrup, molasses-black, congealed at his wounds and run down him in little creeks and streams. He was run through as many times as old Sebastian. His constant slosh had turned to a slurp, mud at the bottom of a played-out well. He was a quart low at least, and he'd lost about six inches in height when he stood. I'd offered to yank those arrows out and sew him up, but he'd waved me off. I think if I did've yanked them, he would uncork entirely and decant on the hardpan and leave nothin' but a deflated suit. Through the faceplate, I couldn't rightly tell if he looked up Godward, or where the hell he looked.

Me, a tomahawk had got me on my left shoulder an' had cutten off some of my ear with it. It was startin' to ripen and fester and I smelled a dark smell comin' up off it, up from under the tincture I'd put on. Smelled like hot grease and death.

John Membraneous was just fine and he rode on up at the head of our posse. His left hand had grown back but not all the way jest now. It only had on it four fingers yet, like those of a baby, and fingernailless so far. But give it another week, I reckoned, and it'd be big enough to take the glove.

We come to the base of a mountain there on the salt flats. The mountain was as red as anything else on the planet, and shattered and jagged and hateful. Membraneous whoahed his jackrabbit to a halt and Choppy and me reined up behind him.

"We're the first," the Venusian said. "We're the first here. We've won."

"*The Sic Semper* crashed into the mountain?"

"No, Mr. Lowell, the mountain *is The Sic Semper.*"

And I looked and I seen that it's so. There was rivets and bolts in the skin of the mountain's faces. Its peaks were twisted, blunted rocket fins, and its vales were the dips between broke machine parts. I seen coils and cogs and ailerons, gigantic in scale and smashed. Up towards its high crags I seen her markings, the *U.S.S. Sic Semper*, in gold filigree, halfway flaked off and upside down and tarnished.

"Misters Lowell and Schiaparelli, our work begins. Let's stake our claim."

We erected notices and beacons all along the base of the mountain, and it took five hours jest to make it around the circumference. The notices established the legal propty rights of John Membraneous, landholder, and those trespassing would be subject to litigation and criminal prosecution unto the furthest extent of the law.

On our rounds, Choppy coughed besides me, a deep, wet, burbling hack from inside him, and more blackness pulsed from out his wounds. On towards evenin', we lit torches and clambered up to a cavern we seen on a low cliff. We left streaks of blood and black pudding and pus on it where we hauled ourselves up the old iron, full of lockjaw. We cussed at it where it cut us.

Inside *The Sic Semper*, we found us some ashes and mummies. We stood in a canyon of 'em, the cold, black cinders up to our knees. Membraneous dug through the drift of 'em with his diseased, baby hand and comes out with a jawbone what's still got three teeth in it, and a gold ring, bent and splayed. He gives the ring to me, calls it my bounty.

"So where's all them pretty fuckin' pictures, you think? Where's the Statue of Liberty?" I said.

"I told you, Mr. Lowell, this expedition was held in order to establish legal claim and to make sure that the legends were true. I am satisfied that they are. This was a simple reconnoitering."

"Simple reconnoitering, huh? I got the rot in my shoulder, Membraneous. It's goin' gangrenous. My pardner's run through thirty're more times. I lost track a how many we killed in gittin' here. And you're satisfied with a dustbowl fulla croakers? You have your satisfaction, have you?"

"You said it yourself concerning New South Hell. Strange rays come out of the ground. Strange rays, Mr. Lowell. If you were hoping to find the treasure of *The Sic Semper* intact, then you were laboring under a misapprehension, but it was through no misleading of mine. But don't worry, the wealth is here and you're still entitled to your five percent. The riches are melted and tortured, but they are here beneath our bootheel. It will take years, decades, to excavate it, but it is indeed here. I am convinced. The mine will yield rich fruit and, should you live, you will be rich men."

"The mine? What mine? Who's gonna mine it? You can't use robots, not in New South Hell. You'll have to use biologicals, and how you gonna git 'em here? It put-near killed us. And even if you do, how you gonna haul the gold out? Can't even git a railroad in here, not through this country."

"All this has been accounted for and you need not worry about the particulars, but as a partial owner in the claim, I will tell you. It will be mined by hand and carried back to civilization by hand. It will be hard labor. Might I borrow your knife, Mr. Lowell?"

I was itchin' to kill him, if I knowed the way. I thought of applying fire, of taking the glue out of him. I took the Bowie knife out of my belt and gave it to him, handle first.

"Thank you. As for the labor force, I saw fit to bring it with me." From the pocket of his duster, he produced the hand I cut off him for McLaren. It twitched still, and since then'd grown a little see-through head on the thumb. The other fingers now had got fingers of their own. It had a stinger, too, a-sproutin' from the wrist stump. It bobbed and weaved.

"The hell's that?" I said.

"This," Membraneous told me, "is the Eight-Thousandth and Fifty-Seventh Clansman of the House of Barboa." He then took my knife and cut off the tip of the dismembered hand's index finger, at the joint, and he threw the fingertip into the ashes around us, it vanished in the black froth and torchlight. "And that was the Eight-Thousandth and Fifty-Eighth Clansman." He proceeded to dicin' up the hand, at the knuckles and the fat of the palm, through the Delta of Venus and the Mound of Mars. My blade slipped through the milkglass flesh like there weren't nothing there. He tossed the pieces, willy-nilly, about us. "The Eight-Thousandth and Fifty-Ninth, The Eight-Thousandth and Sixtieth, John Membraneous the Eight-Thousandth and Sixty-First," he said with each chunk.

I say, "Christ Amighty."

Choppy wheezed next to me.

The cavern we was in's huge, extendin' longer than the light of the flame cut. The south wall swooped above us, on it, row on row, was old earth humans, suspended ass-end up in acceleration chairs, all roped in. They'd gone black and dry, salted like jerky by the winds. They ain't got no eyes no more. Ten thousand sockets looked down on us.

Through the ashes at our feet I hear a skitterin', somethin' rasslin' around in there. I see a pale green slug what used to be Membraneous' knucklebone slide its way up the pock-marked wall and latch itself onto the danglin' leg of one of the mummies. I hear a chewin'.

"There will be enough here for me to eat, to sustain me, I think," the Venusian says. "It is good food, rich food, all these popes and kings. I will grow strong and work the mine myselves. Your duty to me is almost at an end, Misters Schiaparelli and Lowell, at the completion of your last task, you are at your liberty." He handed the Bowie back to me. I touched it like it's hot or's been soiled. He took off his slouch hat and hung it on a splinter of red iron. Then off comes his duster and his vest, his gold watch on a chain and everything down to his boots. He folded them neat in a pile and stood before us naked as anything. I seen his brain hoverin' down where his stomach ought to be, it's deep gray and has triangles comin' up off it.

"You'll have to cut quite small, Mr. Lowell. I think that two hundred of me ought to do. I told you once, I am in need of killers and cruel men. Should you survive your retreat from New South Hell, you may expect dividend cheques from me no later than winter of next year, I should think."

He splayed his arms and legs out. Through the guttering torchlight that wafted through him, I thought I saw the shapes of bats. Choppy is besides me, settin' on a broken coil, still and quiet. I didn't hear no slosh no more. First time in years I heard no slosh. The arrows poked through him, quiverless. We had no food, nor water, nor provisions of any sort. The rabbits was wore-out and skinny. There was strange rays about, and New South Hell is bad country. It's fulla cactus and rattlers. We seen em'. The snakes are striped red and black as Mars. They's a mile long, they encircle the Earth and blot out the sky. My mind was figurin' the odds of us makin' it back to the Rio alive, and the figures I tallied was long damn luck.

I come at him with the knife.

I'd try to make it hurt.

AUTHOR BIOGRAPHIES

Terry Alexander (*Diablo Seven*) lives with his wife Phyllis on a small farm near Porum, Oklahoma. They have three children and eleven grandchildren. Terry has been published in various anthologies from Pro Se Press, Airship 27, Pulp Modern, Metahuman Press, Hazardous Press, Grinning Skull Press and May December Publications. He is a member of the Tahlequah Writers, Ozark Writers League, Oklahoma Writers Federation, and The Fictioneers.

Cecelia Chapman (*The Conservator*) is an American visual artist working in text and video. Her website is ceceliachapman.com.

Harri B. Cradoc (*Have Time Machine, Will Travel*) has written fiction and essays for over thirty years. He studied forensics in a U.S. Air Force program designed to train computer science instructors. After many years as a systems administrator, he now teaches computer programming and has developed his own course in cyber security. His home is in Port Dickinson, New York.

Milo James Fowler (*The Showgirl and the Wendigo*) is a teacher by day and a speculative fictioneer by night. When he's not grading papers, he's imagining what the world might be like in a dozen alternate realities. Over the past 5 years, his short fiction has appeared in more than 100 publications, including *AE SciFi*, *Cosmos*, *Daily Science Fiction*, *Nature*, *Shimmer*, and the *Wastelands 2* anthology. His collection of weird western tales starring Coyote Cal & Big Yap is available wherever books are sold. www.milojamesfowler.com

Joshua Gage (*Junction, Texas*) is an ornery curmudgeon from Cleveland, His first full-length collection, *breaths*, is available from VanZeno Press. *Intrinsic Night*, a collaborative project he wrote with J. E. Stanley, was published by Sam's Dot Publishing. His most recent collection, *Inhuman: Haiku from the Zombie Apocalypse*, is available on Poet's Haven Press. He is a graduate of the Low Residency MFA Program in Creative Writing at Naropa University. He has a penchant for Pendleton shirts, rye whiskey and any poem strong enough to yank the breath out of his lungs.

Walt Giersbach's (*Boomer Boy, You're A Man Now*) fiction has appeared in *Bewildering Stories*, *Big Pulp*, *Connotation Press*, *Corner Club Press*, *Every Day Fiction*, *Everyday Weirdness*, *Gumshoe Review*, *Lunch Hour Stories*, *Mouth Full of Bullets*, *OG Short Fiction*, *Over My Dead Body*, *Paradigm Journal*, *Pif Magazine*, *Pulp Modern*, *Pure Slush*, *r.kv.r.y*, *Rose and Thorn Journal*, *Short Fiction World*, *Short-Story.Me*, *Southern Fried Weirdness*, *The Short Humour Site*, *Wapshott Chronicles*, *The World of Myth*, *Writers Haven and Written Word*. Two volumes of short stories, *Cruising the Green of Second Avenue*, have been published by Wild Child (www.wildchildpublishing.com) and are available from Barnes & Noble, Amazon, and other online book retailers. He served for three decades as director of communications for Fortune 500 companies, helped publicize the Connecticut Film Festival, managed publicity and programs for Western Connecticut State University's Haas Library, and moderates a writing group in New Jersey.

DeAnna Knippling (*Flesh, Blood, Money*) grew up on the Great Plains, a land driven by expansionism, murder, corruption, and just plain good folks. She lives in a time where souls are bought and sold without even the benefit of a piece of paper to mark the exchange. And she'd feel bad for some of the monsters crushed by such things, but they shouldn't have been there in the first place. She lives in Colorado with her husband and daughter, has been published in *Big Pulp*, *Black Static*, *Crossed Genres*, and more.

Her latest book is *Alice's Adventures in Underland: The Queen of Stilled Hearts*. You can find her at www.WonderlandPress.com and Facebook.

Gerri Leen (*Panning in Thin Air*) lives in Northern Virginia and originally hails from Seattle. She has stories and poems published by: *Daily Science Fiction*, *Escape Pod*, *Grimdark*, *Athena's Daughters 2* and others. She is editing an anthology, *A Quiet Shelter There*, which will benefit homeless animals and is due out in 2015 from Hadley Rille Books. See more at http://www.gerrileen.com.

Mike Loniewski (*Siege*) is a writer battling it out in New Jersey. His prose work has been published by *Shotgun Honey*, One Eye Press, *Flash Fiction Offensive*, and NewMyths.com, with upcoming work from Pro Se Press. His comics have been published by Image Comics, DC Comics/Zuda, APE Entertainment, and Alterna Comics. Follow him on twitter at @redfox_write.

Paul Lorello (*Chikcheeree*) is a freelance writer from Ronkonkoma, New York. His fiction has appeared in *Big Pulp*, Big Pulp's *Kennedy Curse* anthology, *Black Chaos: Tales of the Zombie*, *Membrane*, and *Pseudopod*. In 2014, the Pseudopod podcast of Paul's story, "Growth Spurt", was chosen as the winner of the coveted Parsec Award for Best Speculative Fiction Story, Short Form. Paul lives with three quadrupeds and one biped and knows very little about everything.

John Medaille (*Above Snakes*) lives in Dallas, TX. He has been published at *Pseudopod* and *Escape Pod*.

John F.D. Taff (*The Two of Guns*) is the Bram Stoker Award-nominated author of the critically acclaimed novella collection, *The End in All Beginnings*. Taff has been writing dark speculative fiction for 25 years. He has more than 80 stories in publications that include *Cemetery Dance*, *Horror Library V*, The *Hot Blood*

Series, *Shock Rock II*, *Dark Visions - Volume One*, *Ominous Realities*, and *Death's Realm*. His collection of short stories, *Little Deaths*, was well reviewed and named the "No. 1 Horror Collection of 2012" by *HorrorTalk*. His historical ghost novel, *The Bell Witch*, was released in April 2013, and the thriller novel *Kill/Off* was released in December 2013. A standalone novella, *The Sunken Cathedral*, will be published by Grey Matter Press in August 2015. Another novella will be featured in *I Can Taste the Blood*, in addition to work from Erik T. Johnson, J. Daniel Stone, Joe Schwartz and Josh Malerman, coming from Grey Matter in Spring 2016. You can learn more about John from his website at johnfdtaff.com, or follow him on Twitter @johnfdtaff.

Joriah Wood (*The Blood of Family*) is a pseudonym for Christopher Smith. He lives in western Michigan with his wife and three kids, who provide endless sources of both inspiration and distraction. He loves the short-story format and has been published recently in *Big Pulp* and *The Siren's Call*, while continuing to write for the weird west serial anthology *Whiskey and Wheelguns*. He also pens the occasional comic script for *Champion City Comics*.

Peg, slamming something against the broken door, pushed the rotting wood hard into Susan's mask and mouthpiece. Susan fell back, mouthpiece dislodged and bubbling, the mask hanging to her knees. Instinctively, she grabbed for Peg's, but Peg fought back, swinging her fist full force between Susan's legs, then ripping away the line to Susan's tank.

excerpt from *Dead in the Water*
by Janett Grady

The gorilla started towards us, looking less and less like a gentle giant with each stomping step. Her gait was strange. I couldn't recognize a gorilla's normal gait, but it couldn't have been as jerky or as stiffly lumbering as the one advancing upon us. As she grew closer, other odd attributes also became clear: gaping wounds dripping gray ooze, broken fangs, and a sickening stench that distance had been kind enough to keep away until then. Backing away only made her move quicker, and before long, she was a mere ten feet in front of us. It was then that I noticed how much Knight's fear had increased.

"What do we do?" I asked him and he shook his head frightfully.

excerpt from *Test 17*
by Jessica McHugh

M

*Murder &
the Macabre
from* **BIG PULP**

www.ingramcontent.com/pod-product-compliance
Lightning Source LLC
Chambersburg PA
CBHW031954010726
47493CB00007B/2200